Dreams and Glass

Speculations from the Midwest

OF RUST AND GLASS

Dream of Rust and Glass

Edited by Curtis A. Deeter, Shannon Holleran, Leah McNaughton Lederman, Jonie McIntire, and Andrew Reising

© 2021 Of Rust and Glass, LLC

All rights reserved. No part of this publication may be reproduced, stored in a retrieval system, or transmitted in any form or by any means, electronic, mechanical, photocopying, recording or otherwise without the prior permission of the publisher.

This is a work of fiction. Names, characters, businesses, places, events, locales, and incidents are either the products of the author's imagination or used in a fictitious manner. Any resemblance to actual persons, living or dead, or actual events is purely coincidental.

Published by:
Of Rust and Glass
607 River Road
Maumee, OH 43537

Typesetting: Curtis A. Deeter

Cover Art: Nicole Edelbrock
https:// nicoleedelbrock.com

ISBN: 978-1-7367728-5-0

We dedicate this anthology to the dreamers, to the believers, to the people who never stop asking "what if?" Without you, this world would not be half as interesting

About the Cover Artist

Nicole Edelbrock is a graphic designer based in Toledo, Ohio. As well as working as a graphic designer, Nicole is passionate about portrait photography as well as designing unique crowns and headpieces for her company Faeted Creations. With an unlimited arsenal of different mediums, she never stops creating. Nicole enjoys working on 2D, 3D, and digital art from illustrations to wall hangings. On a more personal note, she lives with her black cat & snake and often loves to collaborate with other artists. One of her favorite things to do is trying new locally-owned restaurants whenever possible.

Her cover art stems from her trying to show one's own identity. The work is representative of the duality in all people, but especially stemming from within Geminis. She created it with her own identity in mind, but she loves how open it is for others to interpret, as well. The digital piece is titled, "Identity."

THE BROKEN PLANETARIUM by Madisen L. Ray	1
STARCATCHER by Jessica Weyer Bentley	4
THE JUPITER BOOMERANG by Andrew Reising	5
YOU CAN NEVER GO HOME AGAIN by Andrew Reising	24
TETHERED by Megan Santucci	36
CYANIC SYMPHONY FOR THE GLOVEBOX by Maxwell Gierke	47
SINGULARITY by Leah McNaughton Lederman	49
HEARTWOOD by Chris J. Bahnsen	55
TURBULENT AIRSPACE by Barry Burton	67

COMFORTABLY NUMB 78
    by Tom Barlow

THE PLACES BETWEEN 97
    by Jacob Minasian

FOUR POEMS 104
    by Joshua Gage

TAKE ME TO YOUR LOWENBRAU 109
    by John Bukowski

COMMUNITY OF ME 114
    by Scott D. Peterson

THE TRAIN TO PIPER HOLLOW 128
    by Jen Mierisch

The Broken Planetarium
by Madisen L. Ray

> *Madisen L. Ray works in public relations in Indianapolis, Indiana and holds an English Literature degree from Ball State University. She is an avid gamer and craves stories told in any medium.*

We expected it to have collapsed by now, the dome deflated or dented. Our excitement grows as we approach. *There, is that a curve from the roof? Can you see it? Is it whole?*

We break into a run when we're close enough to see it protruding from the dark brick façade. All precautions are thrown aside as we race to the building and down a short ramp to a pair of metal-frame doors. They are chained shut from the inside, but the glass shattered long ago, its remains nothing more than sparkling dust on the pavement.

Shh, shh, wait, he says, a hand back to keep the rest of us from rushing in. We know the dangers of being reckless—we'd lost one just a few weeks ago. It had looked safe. It had been quiet. But too late we saw the flash, heard the rattle. And they were gone.

He sweeps his flashlight across the gaping doors and into the shadowy hallway beyond. No glassy, shining eyes reflect back at us. It's safe to move in.

We remember the way: Sharp right, down another ramp, take a left into an antechamber, and then through the theater doors. The planetarium.

We step inside and it's like we took our fifth-grade field trip yesterday. We were bused in, bouncing in our seats as we resisted every urge to ask, *Are we there yet?* Single-file lines, hands behind our backs, ushered into a movie theater unlike any we'd ever seen before. The planetarium's smooth screens belied the geometric structure behind it to keep it erect. Down the rows of rickety, cushioned folding seats we stomped, giggling when we sat and leaned back, and back, and back. They didn't shush us right away, enjoying the reclining seats as much as we did. But as the lights dimmed and we started whisper-shrieking to one another, they told us to quiet down and look up.

And we did. And a night sky more beautiful than any we had ever seen before was projected above our heads. *This is the Milky Way. This is the North Star. Can you find Orion by his belt? Where's Leo?* A year's worth of night sky, stargazing from around the world, in ninety tidy minutes.

The lights returned. We sat back up. We walked back into the bright sunshine. We thought we'd never see night skies like that again.

Now we see them every time we look up, a Crack in what our ancestors thought was a massive dome above us. Its edges are frayed and shine sickly silver in the day and muted green at night. Every shooting star makes your heart skip a beat. *When is the next one coming?*

We retreat into the planetarium after a thorough sweep. Nothing under the remaining chairs. Nothing hiding in the projector room. No holes nibbled or scratched into the screen for anything to have found its way into the dome's inner workings. It's quiet. It's dark. We lay back in the reclining seats and look up at the vague gray screen above us.

I can hear her breathing more deeply beside me, falling into a tentative sleep. I realize I can't sleep, not just yet. Not until I check.

I climb the short stairs to the projector room and step inside. The computer screen is dark. No fans hum behind their metal and plastic casings. No lights flicker to indicate the projector works. And yet... I follow the thick cord to the wall. It's not plugged in. We've been surprised by what still works before—some transformers getting a shot of power from a plant that's somehow getting enough solar power through the Crack. An automatic door and freezer here, table lamps and an oven there. It's always worth trying.

So, I try it. I plug the projector in. And it hums to life.

The computer doesn't turn on, but a small panel on the projector lights up, bathing me in artificial blue light. I look out into the planetarium. In the center of the screen, five tidy white letters read *READY*.

I tap the panel. There are a series of pre-programmed scenarios to choose from: *Antarctica, Hawaii, Indianapolis, Serengeti*. But one scenario shines brighter than the others. It simply reads *Noon*. I select it.

The planetarium fills with daylight. The screen is heart-achingly bright, a shade of blue only seen in memories and broken colored pencils. Those who were sleeping lurch awake, startled. *Sorry,* I whisper, because it seems irreverent to break the moment with too much noise. At the bottom edge of the dome are wispy silhouettes of grass and flowers and bees. The unbroken cerulean sky is projected before us. A few clouds float across the screen and away. We stare until our eyes hurt, unused to the brightness, unused to the coolness instead of hazy orange or dusty yellow tainted with a cosmic purple wound.

We stare until the projection starts to fade, the power reserves running dry. The fan slows, the projector clicks, and the screen snaps to black. The panel dims to nothing. It's still and quiet.

I return to my reclining seat. We all fall into a restless sleep, dreaming of clear skies and warm sunshine.

Starcatcher
by Jessica Weyer Bentley

Jessica Weyer Bentley is an author and poet. Her first collection of poetry, Crimson Sunshine, *was published in May of 2020 (AlyBlue Media). Jessica is a contributing writer for several books in the award-winning Grief Diaries Series. She has been anthologized in the 2020 Women of Appalachia,* Women Speak Series Vol. 6, *also in the 2020 edition of the journal* Common Threads, *by the Ohio Poet's Association and in the Highland Park Summer Muse Series* Anthology of Shoes. *Jessica resides in Northwest, Ohio.*

Your ghost is forever my shadow,
Peter Pan in olive tights.
I burn to fly with you away,
far away from these old rooms.
I cannot grow; stifled by a fractured memory.
Stunted infinitely by your absence.
There are no mermaids or pirate ships.
No fairy dust or Indian Maidens.
Only fake smiles and worn-out stories.
Love dies here like fairies succumbing to white lies and stiff suits.
I step to the edge now pausing to glimpse the clock.
The hour chimes a gruesome tune.
The marble slides beneath my Chenille socks.
 I take a breath staring out to the Prussian blue.
Second star to the right and straight on till morning.

The Jupiter Boomerang
by Andrew Reising

Andrew Reising is the writer and creator of Wild Speculation, *a speculative fiction anthology podcast. He lives in Toledo, Ohio with his wife and two children.*

Jaylen's father looked up as she burst into the hangar.

"Dad, please tell me you did not just bet everything on this race. What about the business? What about mom? How could you do this?!"

He had just been speaking to the mechanics working on her racing ship, and she knew airing her grievances in front of the employees would embarrass him, but she wanted him embarrassed. He was jeopardizing everything.

He couldn't even meet her eyes.

"Jaylen, honey, let's go somewhere private, and I'll explain—"

"No, dad. You stand there and explain it to me now."

Jaylen saw his discomfort, and took a malicious thrill from it. She knew this was childish, but she was angry! And besides, hadn't her father started the childish behavior by betting the entire family fortune on a single race?

Her father's shoulders sagged.

"Fine. You want to know the truth, Jay? The business is failing. The last three asteroids we mined didn't have as many raw resources as the materials surveys promised. So, for the past six months, no one has contracted us to mine any more, despite having several with promising surveys.

People think we're doctoring the surveys to get contracts. And I can't afford to bankroll a mining operation myself.

"I only have enough money to keep the business open for another three months."

Guilt flooded Jaylen. She should have let her father move the conversation elsewhere. Now a glance around the room at the mechanics' startled faces made clear that they just realized their jobs might be in jeopardy.

"I'm...sorry, dad. Let's talk in private."

Jaylen let him lead her into an office. After he closed the door, she slumped into a chair.

"Why didn't you tell me, dad?! Why am I even in this race right now? The fuel cost alone must be astronomical, not to mention the entry fee and paying those guys for labor and retrofit. We could have skipped the race."

"No." Her father's voice was unexpectedly steely. "No, this has been your dream since you were little. The Jupiter Boomerang race is the biggest race in the system, and only happens every seven and a half years. I wasn't about to let you miss this."

"But...what about the business? Your employees? What about mom? How are we going to pay for her treatments?"

Jaylen's mom had been sick for years with a rare autoimmune disorder. She had to live in a clean room most of the time, but an experimental treatment allowed her the occasional excursion back into the world and the occasional thoroughly cleaned visitor into hers. But both the treatment and the clean room residence were expensive.

"Don't worry about all that, honey. Everything will be fine. If things don't work out with this race, I have a buyer ready to take over the business. She's been wanting to buy out a prospecting company for a while, so she can take care of that in-house. The employees will continue to work, and the pay-out will be enough for your mom and me to live on for years, even without another source of income.

"The biggest thing is you and your racing career. The *Swordfish IV* is yours. If you can find a patron, you can keep racing. If not, you might have to sell her. She'll get you a hefty sum on her own. Then, a pilot with your reputation should have no trouble finding work. But if this really is your last race, I wanted to make sure you were able to run the Boomerang before calling it quits."

"But…why did you bet all that money on this race? This is my first time in the majors. I'm a good pilot, but I'm going up against the best! Surely, it would have been better to hold onto that money?"

Her father shrugged.

"I split it into two equal bets. The first one was a 'win' bet on you. The odds are pretty steep against you winning, so if you do, I'll have enough to keep the business, and even bankroll a mining operation or two myself.

"The second one is in your name. It's a 'show' bet, with odds at 5 to 1. You get at least third in this race, you'll earn enough to enter another race or two, even without a patron. And if you place that high, the potential patrons will be lining up."

He must have seen Jaylen tense, because he continued.

"It was my choice, dear. Regardless of the outcome of this race, I am proud of you. Don't worry about the bets. Just do the best you can, and have an amazing time. You're in the Boomerang!"

Jaylen smiled at her father, genuinely excited, but anxious about the responsibility he had put on her with those bets.

Markus was shaken. Had he really just heard the boss tell his daughter he was going bankrupt? What would that mean for Markus' job?

At least I'm finding out now, while I can do something about it.

He finished sealing the panel he was working on, then stood up and stretched.

"Gonna go hit the head," he said to the other mechanics. A few grunted acknowledgement, but most ignored him, focusing on their work.

In the restroom, he pulled up the anonymous message he had received on his tablet the night before:

Mr. Markus Ritter:

It has come to our attention that you are a mechanic contracted to work on Jaylen Felling's Swordfish IV.

It has also come to our attention that you have racked up significant gambling debts.

It would please us greatly to be able to know with certainty that Ms. Felling will come in last place or be unable to finish the Boomerang.

If you have the means and desire to make that happen, please contact us at the number below, and we will arrange to wipe out your debts.

If you decide not to help us, erase this message and go about your life.

If you decide to show this message to the authorities, you will find all of your debts suddenly and urgently called due, forcefully if necessary. None of us want that.

We hope to hear from you.

Your friends at Belt-515-824.

If I'm about to be out of a job, I've gotta find some way to pay these debts.

Markus called the number from the message.

After the second ring, just as he was starting to second-guess his decision, someone answered.

"Hello?"

"Um, Hi. This is Markus Ritter?"

"Ah, yes! We were starting to wonder if we would hear from you, Mr. Ritter. So does this mean you've decided to take us up on our offer?"

"Y-yes. I'll take the job."

"Good! You must find a way to sabotage her ship so that the malfunction looks like an accident. But it must be non-lethal."

"Non-lethal? We're talking about spaceships here. Even a tiny malfunction can trigger a lethal cascade. I can't promise—"

"This is non-negotiable, Mr. Ritter. If anything happens to the girl, our deal is off, and you will be reported to the authorities. Understand?"

"I… understand."

After her talk with her father, Jaylen asked the mechanics to give her a little time alone with her ship so she could inspect their work. They were professionals, and great people, but it always made Jaylen feel better to know the condition of everything on the *Swordfish IV*.

"Well, girl, this might be our last race together. You ready?" Jaylen murmured as she inspected the fuel lines. "This'll be our longest race yet, so I'm relying on you more than ever. I can't very well stay at the controls for a week straight. Can I count on you, girl?"

A lot of The Boomerang was determined before the race ever started. Pilots and their teams plotted trajectories, planned fuel burns, and calculated a host of variables. During the flight itself, the pilot would make course corrections to shave off time or deal with unexpected complications.

Jaylen and the *Swordfish IV* had been racing together since she was 13, when she became the youngest pilot ever to qualify for the Lagrange race back near Earth. Now, six years later, she knew the ship so well, she could identify something wrong by sight, or even by feel.

She was just noticing that something looked off about the ventral thrusters when one of the mechanics returned. Halting, he glanced around, apparently noticing that none of the other techs were there.

"I-I'm sorry, miss. I didn't realize—"

Jaylen waved his apology away. "No worries. You're Markus, right?"

The mechanic nodded hesitantly.

"Well, Markus, something seems off about these thrusters. Could you go over them extra thoroughly before the race? I'd be in big trouble if those crapped out on me during The Boomerang."

Jaylen smiled at the nervous young mechanic, trying to put him at ease. She'd known some of the older mechanics for years, but this Markus had been hired only six months ago, and she hadn't gotten to know him yet.

"Of course, miss! I'll get on that right away!"

But he barely made eye contact with Jaylen as he turned quickly to find the tools he'd need for the repairs.

Leaving the hangar, Jaylen shook her head.

So much for putting him at ease. *If I do well enough that this race isn't my last, I really need to sit down with Markus and anyone else on the crew I don't know well. They deserve that.*

Back in his room, Markus let out a nervous laugh he'd been holding in all day.

I was so worried I wouldn't be able to sabotage the ship in a way that'd look like an accident, but without injuring the pilot. But then, the Princess Pilot herself points out the faulty thrusters, and the rest just falls into place!

He sank into a chair and called one of his drinking buddies.

"Hello?"

"Hey, Hank! It's Markus. I've got an inside scoop on the race tomorrow."

"Yeah? Well, why you telling me?"

"My credit's a bit tapped right now, but I've got a big pay-out coming soon."

"I'm not gonna throw you a line that you plan on paying back with winnings, Markus. Winnings that'll probably never come, the way your luck goes."

"No, man, the pay-out is for a job. I'm good for it! Just put a K down for me—"

"A K?! You expect me to float you that much?!"

"Yeah. I do. Because this is a genuine scoop. Put a K down for me and however much you want for you."

"What's the bet?"

"You're gonna put it all on shorting the *Swordfish IV*."

"The *Swordfi*...That's the Felling girl's ship. Don't you work for them?"

"Like I said. It's a sure thing."

Hank paused a moment before responding, and Markus worried that maybe his buddy was a little more scrupulous than he had thought.

"Okay, Markus, it's a deal—"

Markus relaxed.

"—but if this goes bust, I'm coming after you for your full K and half of mine, too, got it?"

Markus smiled. "I got it. Don't worry Hank; this time next week, we'll both be flush."

"Hey, kid, welcome to the big leagues!"

Liam hailed Jaylen over her comms as they waited for the race to start.

"You're not much older than I am Liam."

"Yeah, yeah, don't get too big a head. You started winning those little races after I left, and you don't stand a chance here. Especially in that little sloop."

She could hear the smirk in his voice.

The two had raced a dozen times, she had only beat him once, and he had blamed that loss on a technical malfunction. But she wanted him to take her seriously.

"The odds makers seem to think I stand a chance."

"That's because people like betting on the shiny new racer. The truth is, the last you'll see of us 'til after the race will be our engine plumes."

"We'll see about that."

Jaylen cut the line. Liam was getting under her skin, and she couldn't afford that. She needed all her concentration to pull off her plan.

The *Swordfish IV* could compete with those bigger ships, if the changes to her engine worked. And if she could make the necessary adjustments on the fly. And if everything else worked out...

Two days into the race, Jaylen passed her first competitor. By the fourth day, approaching Jupiter, she had passed all but three of the other ships. The extended run under low thrust had worked.

Jaylen hailed Liam, one of the three pilots she was still trailing.

"Hey Liam, I see you! Is the race over already?"

At first there was no response, and Jaylen thought he was ignoring her.

"Hey, kid. I gotta admit, you are doing a hell of a lot better than I expected. Still, that constant burn had to eat through your fuel stores. We'll leave you behind on the way back."

"We'll see about that."

Jaylen watched the three ships ahead of her angle their trajectory to catch the gravity well of the gas giant.

In her smaller ship she could take the turn faster without being thrown out of the partial orbit of the planet.

She angled her ship so Jupiter looked like it was above her and aimed her ship just above the atmosphere.

Jaylen could feel Jupiter's gravity grabbing her ship, a small tug pressing her down in her seat. As she made the turn, the sensation grew. Still, it wasn't anything she couldn't handle.

It was…a lot of pressure though…it made her want to…close…her…eyes…

Jaylen forced her eyes open. This turn shouldn't have this much force in it. She checked her screens, and, sure enough, she had come into her turn too quickly. If she didn't make an adjustment, she would be slung out of Jupiter's orbit too soon, heading in the wrong direction.

Still, it wasn't a huge problem. She fired off her ventral thrusters, keeping the *Swordfish IV's* nose aimed at the horizon.

This'll eat up some fuel, but I'll come out of the slingshot faster, so I should be good.

She might actually come out ahead because of this. Jaylen let out a giggle as she tore past the three larger ships and took the lead.

I might actually win this thing! Dad might get to keep the business! I'll get to keep raci...

The ventral thrusters sputtered and died.

What?! No, no, no, no! I thought that mechanic, Markus, fixed those!

Trying to hold the arc she was in, Jaylen rolled the ship, firing the dorsal thrusters.

As she did, her blood rushed to her head. Her vision started to dim.

Got...to...get...this....set...

Jaylen typed commands to the ship: Shut off the dorsal thrusters. Gun the main engines. Do both...here. She marked the point to put them on track for the return. Then she let her eyes close.

"Counting on you...girl...don't...let me down... now..."

And she drifted into unconsciousness.

"Hey! Hey, kid! You there? Jaylen!"

Waking up to a headache and Liam's voice was not Jaylen's idea of a good time.

"What do you want, Liam?"

"Hey, that was an awesome slingshot maneuver you pulled, kid, but you're veering way off-course. Are you okay?"

She jolted up.

"What?! How did that..."

The ship was attempting to fly as normal, under thrust from the main engines, with micro-corrections from the various thrusters.

Except, every ventral thruster was shot. The nose of her ship was aiming into dead space. The first three ships had passed her, and several more would, soon.

"Are you okay, Jaylen? Do you need me to contact a rescue ship?"

She heard genuine concern in his voice.

"No. No, I'll be fine. Thanks, though. Go win this one for me."

"Okay, if you're sure."

"Focus on the race, old-timer."

"You got it, kid."

The connection clicked off.

The nickname didn't rankle this time. He had been the only ship to contact her as she veered off-course.

"But now, we've got to find a way to get back, girl. Even if we can't win, we've got to finish our last race under our own power."

And she set to work calculating a way to use the remaining thrusters to get her back.

Markus sighed with relief. He had worried that Jaylen would somehow manage to correct for the lost thrusters, and win the race. Then, when her ship had started listing out of its path, he had worried that she had an accident, and his anonymous partners would out him to the authorities.

But the *Swordfish IV* was obviously working to correct course, so the girl must be okay. And he had just become filthy stinkin' rich.

He called Hank.

"You crazy idiot. I was starting to think you fed me a dud."

"Well, hello to you, too, Hank." Markus smiled.

"She was in first place, and I was like, 'there's no way every other ship will pass her,' but then those thrusters gave out, and I knew that would slow her down. But how did you get her to veer off-course?"

Markus, chagrined that his friend had realized the blown thrusters would slow her even if they didn't throw her out of the slingshot, decided to play coy.

"I don't know what you're talking about."

"Come on, man! You gotta tell me! Did you tamper with her onboard computers? Why did it take her so long to correct after that maneuver?"

Satisfied that he had Hank enraptured, Markus told him his guess.

"My first thought was, when the ventral thrusters blew, she'd be thrown out of orbit too early, and have to spend extra time and fuel to get back in the race. Then, she rolled the ship and used her dorsal thrusters to keep on course! But all that pressure was pulling blood into her head. So my guess is she passed out while pulling that maneuver.

"She's awake again, correcting course. But it's too late. The rest of the ships will overtake her."

"But...how did you get those thrusters to blow at just the right moment?"

"That was easy. I just weakened the connections so that they'd blow out at a certain burn threshold. She reached that threshold sooner than I expected, because she came into Jupiter's orbit too fast."

"Huh. Wow. Well, it looks like you were right. She's gonna come in last."

"I told you it was a sure thing!"

"Talk to you later."

"Yeah see you—"

But the line was dead. Markus looked down at the comm.

Weird. Hank seemed excited about my plan, but then he just...didn't? But why? He's going to be rich, too.

But Markus' attention was soon back on the race feed. Jaylen was getting back on-course.

Jaylen could easily plot a course back to Ceres, but the still-functioning thrusters would need almost all her remaining fuel to keep on course. So she would definitely be the last ship to cross the finish line.

It also meant that she would be cruising in null-g most of the way, except for the occasional course corrections which would roll the ship, then temporarily give her a 'down' direction pointed anywhere but at her feet.

Gritting her teeth, Jaylen inputted the navigation directions.

"Come on, old girl. Let's finish this race with our head held high."

In the end, Jaylen crossed the finish line less than two hours after the second to last ship. The course correction maneuvers made her nauseated during the first day, but after that, she grew used to them.

After crossing the finish-line, Jaylen used her remaining fuel to slow the *Swordfish IV* and return to dock, her tank as perilously close to empty as she'd ever had it.

She stayed in her seat for a minute, eyes closed, not yet ready to face her father and whoever else had come to greet her.

"We made it, girl. We ran the Jupiter Boomerang. It's more than most people can say, right?"

She opened her eyes. On the monitor, people were gathered outside the ship, including her father, frantically waving his arms.

"I guess I better go see what's up, girl. I'll be back to check out those blown thrusters. Thank you for getting us home."

Rising stiffly, she bent and stretched, letting her body readjust to gravity, even if it was only the microgravity of Ceres. When she opened the hatch, several reporters began shouting.

"What happened with the—"
"—you manage that—"
"—going to do now?"

Jaylen ignored them, climbed down from the hatch, and made her way to her father. As he wrapped her in a hug, she let her tension drain away. Around them, cameras flashed.

"Oh, darling, I'm so proud of you."

Jaylen pulled back and looked at her father, trying to hold back tears

"Dad, I lost. I came in dead last. You'll have to sell the company, I'll have to quit racing, and…"

She buried her face in his shoulder.

"About that. Come with me. I have someone you need to talk to."

Confused, Jaylen let her father lead her away from the crowd.

Markus checked the address of the bar that Hank had texted to him, went in, and saw his friend sitting in a corner.

Smiling, he sat down opposite Hank.

"So, how much did we win? Feel free to take your K out of my cut."

"We didn't win anything."

Markus jerked upright.

"What?! What do you mean? We placed a bet shorting the *Swordfish IV* and it crossed the finish-line last! We should be rich!"

"Except, I didn't place the bet."

Markus stared in confusion.

"But…why did you…you lied?"

A hand came down on Markus' shoulder.

"Markus Ritter, you are under arrest."

As Jaylen followed her father out of the hangar, someone called to her.

"Excuse me, Miss Felling? I need just a moment of your time."

Her father turned around with his 'business face' on.

"I'm sorry, Miss Felling has a very important meeting, but if you wish to make an appointment, you can—"

"I'm with the Ceres Colony Police, Mr. Felling, and I need to speak with her briefly. It'll just take a moment."

Jaylen could see her father's impatience, so she put a hand on his arm and smiled to let him know it was okay.

"Alright, Officer, but make it quick, please."

"If you could just…" And he led Jaylen and her father into a side room.

Once the door was closed, the officer seemed to relax.

"Miss Felling, what do you know about a mechanic named Markus Ritter?"

Jaylen was surprised.

"Um, he's a newer mechanic on my ship's maintenance crew. Why?"

"Can you tell me anything else about him?"

Jaylen shrugged. "Not really. I haven't spoken to him much, except for right before the race when I asked him to take a look at those thrusters. I guess he missed something."

The officer smiled sadly.

"No, Miss Felling. He didn't miss anything. He deliberately sabotaged your ship, then tried to get his friend to place a bet for him shorting you in the race.

"Luckily, that friend decided to inform us instead of going along with the scheme.

"We have Mr. Ritter in custody, and will be charging him with Sabotage Endangering a Life and with Illegal Gambling.

"Your testimony will help insure his conviction, so you will be asked to testify if this goes to trial. Just be aware of that."

Jaylen sat, stunned. Markus had sabotaged her ship? But…why?

Her father, seeing her confusion and distress, spoke up.

"We'll make sure she's available to testify if it comes to that, Officer. Now, if there's nothing else, we really do have a meeting to get to."

"Of course."

The police officer held the door for them as they left the room.

"If you can think of any other useful information, be sure to give us a call down at the station."

He tapped his tablet against Jaylen's, and the police station's contact information appeared on her screen.

"She will, sir," her father said as he rushed her down the hall.

"Look, I was put up to it! I was blackmailed! They held my gambling debts over my head."

Since he hadn't actually made the illegal bet, maybe that charge wouldn't stick. As for the sabotage, maybe if he could give them his blackmailers, they'd let him off easy.

"Do you have proof of this, Markus?"

"There's a message on my tablet from two days before the race. It was sent anonymously, but you guys can track that, right?"

The officer held out Markus' tablet, and Markus entered in the passcode. After a moment, the officer looked up suspiciously.

"I don't see any anonymous message here. Are you sure?"

"Yes!" Markus tried to keep calm. "It was the day before I overheard about the Felling business going under. That news was what pushed me to go along with the scheme."

"There's no message here. Did they give you any other way to contact them?"

"A comm number...let me think..." Markus closed his eyes and pictured the call pad on his comm. "Belt-five-one-five...eight-two...five? No, a four. Eight-two-four."

The officer punched the number into his comm.

"We're sorry. The number you have dialed is not in service at this time. If you would like to—"

"Are you sure that's the right number?"

"Yeah." Markus slumped in his seat. "Is there any way you can figure out who had that number over a week ago?"

The officer shrugged. "I can try, but it's probably a burner account. We're gonna need more than that to get a lead on whoever put you up to this."

"But...you believe me, right? That I was set up?" Markus looked into the officer's eyes, hoping to find some compassion there, and was surprised when he found it.

The officer leaned forward. "Yeah, I believe you. That was a big risk for a single bet, so it makes sense that there was more at stake for you than just that.

"But it doesn't matter what I believe. You sabotaged a ship in one of the most important races in the system. If you can't give us the people who put you up to it, you're gonna be nailed to the wall. So you best remember if there's any lead you can give us."

The officer left the interrogation room, and Markus let himself cry, despair washing through him.

When they arrived at the meeting, Jaylen was surprised to see Liam and an older woman there.

"Uh, hi Liam...What's all this about? Dad seemed really eager to get here."

Liam smiled. "Hey, Jaylen. That was some crazy good flying out there. My patron, Ms. Lydia Thorpe, of Thorpe Refineries, wanted to meet you."

The older woman smiled.

"I wanted to congratulate you, dear. Liam may have won the race, but it is your performance that people will be talking about for years."

"Um...thank you?" Bewildered, Jaylen looked at her father. "What's all this about, Dad?"

"Ms. Thorpe is the friend I told you about, who's buying out the company. She is also a big racing enthusiast, and after what you did...well, I'll let you tell her, Lydia."

"Yes, well, you're father explained to me how you might be in need of a patron, so I would like to extend you the opportunity to join my stable."

"Wait, you want me to..." Jaylen looked from Ms. Thorpe to Liam and back again. "What would that mean for races?"

"We'd race both you and Liam when they allow multiple entries from a single stable, and race you according to your strengths in the races that don't." Ms. Thorpe smiled. "If you decide to join us, I will have both the top young racers in the game, and Thorpe Stables will be dominant for years to come. What do you say?"

Jaylen took a deep breath. This was the dream; a professional racer in a top-tier stable. Still...

"I have one condition."

Ms. Thorpe waved her hand indulgently. "Name it."

"I race with my ship. The *Swordfish IV*."

Ms. Thorpe wrinkled her nose. "Oh, my dear, that model is getting old, and isn't really built for major races," her eyes flicked to Jaylen's father and back to Jaylen, "but I'll tell you what. Bring the old girl with you, and we will get it as racing-fit as we can, and see if we can make it work, alright?"

Jaylen nodded. "Okay."

Ms. Thorpe visibly relaxed. "Good. Now, Liam? Will you take young Jaylen over to the stable offices and walk her through everything?"

"Sure thing, ma'am." Liam smiled at Jaylen as he led her out of the room.

"Kinda weird, the idea of being on the same team, isn't it?"

"Not really." Jaylen smiled back. "That just means every single practice run is another opportunity for me to beat you, old-timer."

Liam laughed. "Good luck with that, kid."

When Jaylen and Liam had left the room, Jeremiah Felling turned to Lydia Thorpe.

"I told you my daughter would impress you. It's not fatherly bias when I say she's good."

Lydia nodded. "Almost too good. If she was any better, she would have managed to avoid coming in last. And that was a very large bet we placed shorting her."

Jeremiah cleared his throat. "Speaking of which, I just received word that the police have arrested Mr. Ritter. Are you sure he can't be traced to us?"

Lydia waved her hand. "Very sure. A reliable contact inside the police department scrubbed our message off Ritter's tablet, and the comm number can't be traced. We're in the clear."

Jeremiah relaxed. "Well, in that case, what do we have left to do?"

Lydia held out her tablet. "Sign at the bottom."

He signed the digital document with his finger.

"There! Now Felling Prospecting is a subsidiary of Thorpe Refineries, and you my dear Jeremiah, are the proud owner of ten percent of Thorpe, as well as of a large cash sum that was just deposited into your Earthside account. Now, I'll take good care of your daughter. You run home and tell that sick wife of yours that everything's going to be fine. Everybody wins!"

"Except for Ritter."

Lydia shrugged. "Everyone who matters wins."

You Can Never Go Home Again
by Andrew Reising

"...any survivors, then hopefully someone will find this one day, and—"

"I got it! It's recording, I think. I've never used a cassette before; this tech is nearly a century old. When we're done, we better play it back to see if it even worked."

"Alright, then, here we go.

"Hello, I am communication specialist Major Eddie Thane of the UN-NASA research ship *Lorentz*. I and the crew of the *Lorentz* are searching the city of Orlando, Florida, for any sign of human life.

"If we don't find anyone in Orlando, we intend to make our way north towards Washington, DC, but we may stop before then if we find anyone who...well, anyone at all. If you are listening to this, please come find us.

"We have been on an experimental mission studying time dilation. When we got back into Earth-orbit, we attempted to hail both Canaveral and Houston, but only got radio silence. So, we opened our hail across all bandwidths, civilian and military, but still got no response.

"Luckily, our pilot and techs were able to get us down safely without ground support.

"Ground control and the air force base appeared to be completely abandoned, so we made our way into the city .So far we have found no one. But we did find this large collection of old audio cassette tapes and Walkman cassette players, which we will leave as markers of our passage. Where are we leaving them?"

"People will be looking for supplies to survive this. We should leave them in the canned goods sections of stores. With the beans. We'll want a store that we'll find all the way up to DC, so we'll leave them in Walmarts."

"Alright. The next city where we leave the tapes will be Jacksonville. We'll leave a tape with a Walkman in each of the first three Walmarts we find along the highway.

"If I'm being completely honest, this is starting to freak us out. If you find this and have any way of broadcasting a radio signal, please try to get through to us, if you can. Please tell us what happened here, even if you don't follow us north.

"We are making this recording on April 12, 2094, according to this digital watch we found in our search.

"I don't know what happened, but if you are still alive, please stay safe.

"How was that?"

"Good. We'll just play it to make sure it worked, then make a few copies and place them in Walmarts around the city."

"Can you believe it's April?"

"Two whole months later than we thought. I wonder how—"

"—should be working, so whenever you're ready."

"Okay. Hello. I am Major Eddie Thane, communications specialist on the crew of the *UN-NASA Lorentz*, a research vessel designed to run time dilation experiments. It took us four days to get to Jacksonville, so the date should be April 16, 2094.

"If you listened to our cassette in Orlando, then you know what happened; we returned to Earth to find everything abandoned, not a trace of other humans, living or dead.

"We're moving north, and we still haven't found anyone.

Our pilot, Lieutenant Samantha Grath, had family in St. Augustine, so we stopped there. It was an eerie experience. We found their house, just as it had been. There were still pictures of her aunt and uncle on the walls, and their belongings were in the drawers. There was no sign of any panic, struggle, or effort to pack up and leave. Their car was even parked in the driveway.

"Whatever happened, people had no time to prepare. Is anyone alive? Did everyone leave and take nothing with them? These are the questions we are trying to answer.

"If you find this tape, please make contact with us. We are starting to worry that we are alone on this planet. We have a ham radio with its signal boosted as far as it will go. We're continuing north towards DC.

"We'll leave our next tape in the first three Walmarts along the highway in Savannah, Georgia. The canned goods section again, with the beans.

"Anything else I forgot?"

"The cars don't—"

"Oh, right. Um, we have discovered that none of the vehicles here work. Even a car in perfect condition with a full tank of gas, it simply will not start. Is this some effect of whatever made the people disappear? Or is it something different? If you know the answer, or if you know a way to get vehicles to work, we would love to hear from you. We'd love to hear from you anyway, since it would mean we aren't alone, but, and now I'm rambling.

"Anyway, northward to Savannah, and we hope to hear from someone soon."

"Okay, let's get this copied and distributed, and then let's—"

"Is it on?"

"Yep."

"This is, once again, Major Eddie Thane of the UN-NASA ship *Lorentz*, and I am recording this message ten days after our arrival back on Earth, so April 22, 2094, if the watch we found is correct. As you may already know from our earlier tapes, I and the rest of the *Lorentz* crew returned from our mission testing the effects of time dilation on humans, to find that everyone seems to have just vanished.

"We are making our way from Orlando to Washington, DC. We're hoping someone there managed to get to a bunker and survive this. And even if not, we might find some clue as to what the hell this is.

"On our way north from Jacksonville, our engineer, Sergeant Alexei Kozlov, reported seeing shadows move out of the corners of his eyes. But whenever he tried to look directly at them, nothing was there. Soon, the rest of us noticed the same thing, but no matter how hard we tried, we could not locate the source of the movement.

"Is something out there, tracking us, while staying out of our direct sight? Is this the same thing that caused everyone to disappear? Or are we just going crazy with paranoia?

"Both options are bad, and, frankly, I don't know which is worse.

"Either way, if you get this message, be careful out there. There might be something in the shadows.

"We are out of cassette tapes and Walkmans, so we're gonna try to find some here in Savannah before we move on. Then we'll be taking things slower as we continue north. In the case you're following us, whoever you are, we want to give you a chance to catch up. And, frankly, I don't think any of us are eager to reach DC, since it's looking more and more likely that it'll be empty there, too—and then what do we do?

"Our next cassette drop will be in Columbia, South Carolina. As always, in the canned goods sections of the first three Walmarts we find.

"I desperately hope that by then we'll have found someone, or you'll have found us."

"Jeez, Eddie, depressing much?"

"Look, I'm not saying anything the crew doesn't know already. And we've got to make peace with the possibility that these tapes might not be found for a long, long time - if they are found at all."

"You really need to snap out of it, or someone else might have to—"

"So I just, okay. Um.

"Greetings. This is Captain Nathaniel Wuthers of the crew of the *UN-NASA Lorentz*. I have taken over the duties of our comm specialist Major Eddie Thane, who is, um, indisposed.

"It is May 4, 2094 as of this recording, and we continue to make progress towards Washington, DC, through this barren landscape that is now Earth.

"We will continue north at this slower pace, to allow anyone who finds these messages to catch up with us, and join us in our efforts of survival.

"Our next cassette drop will be in Raleigh, North Carolina in the first three Walmarts we find.

"Is there anything else?"

"Canned—"

"Right! You will find the tape in with the canned beans. Until then—"

"Tell them about the radio and the animals."

"Why? Aren't these messages just us trying to connect with other survivors?"

"But the information might help—oh just let me…

"Hello, this is Major Anya Novak. I have been assisting Major Thane and now Captain Wuthers with these recordings.

"Before we end this recording, there is some more information we've found that might help you.

"First, we have not seen a single animal on our journey north. It appears that whatever caused the humans to disappear affected other animals, too. Plants and fungi are still here, though. We aren't quite sure what this means.

"Second, we have started to pick up signals on our radio. Just blasts of sound, like music sped up past the point of intelligibility. These sounds fade in then fade out again very quickly, as if the source of the signal is moving past us at high speed. We can't find any kind of pattern in these signals, but they do seem to be slowly increasing in frequency. We're hoping we can figure out what they are, but for now, we don't have a clue.

"As the Captain said, look for our next tape in Raleigh."

"Major, was that really necessary—"

"Yes, Captain. That information could be helpful to whoever finds this, even if they don't follow us north."

"But we want them to follow us north."

"Yeah, but we can't be hoarding information in the face of—"

"Hello. This is Major Eddie Thane of the UN-NASA ship *Lorentz*.

"This is the latest in a series of tapes we have made and left for other survivors on our journey to Washington, DC.

"We've all but given up hope that anyone will find these tapes or find us, but maybe the information will at least help you figure out what the hell happened.

"Captain Wuthers, who insisted on doing the last recording when he thought my messages were getting too dire, is unfortunately no longer with us. He just got up and left a few nights ago, without telling anyone. We found footprints outside the house we were staying in, taking no supplies. Did he leave for the same reason everyone else left? Or did the stress just get to him, and he wandered off? We aren't sure.

"All we know is, we were unable to find him.

"I lost count of the days since we were in Columbia, but I think I'm recording this around May 19, 2094.

"We made another discovery on this leg of our journey: the moving shadows we keep catching glimpses of seem to be more than just figments of our paranoid imaginations. They seem to be somehow connected to the weird radio bursts we pick up.

"Any time we all start seeing those moving shadows in our peripheral vision, the radio burst almost always follows immediately. Then the shadows recede after the radio burst passes.

"We still have no idea what is causing the shadows or the radio bursts. But we did notice that both happen more when we are in or near cities and towns. What does it mean? What is causing them? And are they connected with what made everyone else disappear?

"We don't know. We are still holding out hope that we can find some answers, or better yet, people, in DC.

"Look for our next tape in Richmond, Virginia. As always, you'll find them with the canned beans in the first three Walmarts along the highway."

"You do realize the captain probably just walked off to find a quiet place to blow his brains out, right?"

"Don't say stuff like that while we're still record—"

"I hope somebody finds these damn things."

"It's on, Eddie."

"Why didn't you--fine. Hello, this is Major Eddie Thane. I am part of what's left of the crew of the *UN-NASA*

Lorentz, making our way through this depopulated hellscape from our landing site in Florida up to Washington DC.

"This is a warning to whoever finds this tape: Stay out of the middle of the road.

"Apparently, the radio bursts we have detected come from some sort of mostly invisible force that can interact with the physical world.

"This force is lethal, as we found out the hard way. It slammed into several of our crew members, killing them on impact. It might have killed us all if we hadn't realized that we were safe as long as we stayed off the road. Since then we've stuck to sidewalks, medians, and shoulders, and no one else has been killed.

"Is this what happened to everybody? If so, where are the dead bodies? Because it turned our friends into gruesome splatters, but it didn't make them disappear.

"There are three of us left: Lieutenant Grath, Major Novak, and myself. Hopefully, we will find other survivors in DC and stop there. If we don't find anyone, we'll make more tapes and continue north to New York.

"If we make more tapes, you'll find them with the canned beans in DC area Walmarts.

"I hope this helps you avoid the tragedy we have had to face. And I really hope we find someone in Washington.

"Good luck."

"This is Major Anya Novak. I am the sole surviving member of the crew of the *UN-NASA Lorentz*.

"The mysterious force that is heralded by moving shadows and a radio signal burst has killed the rest of our crew.

"Lieutenant Grath and Major Thane were attempting to cross the interstate highway as we entered DC, when my radio picked up about a dozen signal bursts in quick succession. Before I knew it, Samantha and Eddie were dead, broken bodies splayed out on the road. And I couldn't even risk trying to retrieve their bodies to bury them.

"On top of that, our effort has turned out to be for nothing. There is no one here in DC. For all I know, I am the only living human left on Earth.

"I'm only making one copy of this tape, and won't be making any more after this. I'm done with this shit.

"If I'm still alive, you'll find me in Boston. Boston was my home before all this, so maybe it can be again. I don't know.

"These tapes were probably just as pointless as our journey to DC, but maybe some aliens will discover them in the distant future and figure out what happened to humanity.

"Anyway, meet me in Boston if you find this tape. Or don't. Can't bring myself to care one way or the other."

"This was the seventh and final tape, found in the canned goods section of a DC area Walmart. As it says in the recording, this was the only copy of this final tape ever found.

"Over the past year, avid '*Lorentz* hunters' as they call themselves, have regularly scoured the canned food sections of the Walmarts in every city between Washington, DC, and Boston, but no other tapes were ever discovered.

"When copies of the first tape were found around the city of Orlando, two months after the expected return of the UN-NASA *Lorentz*, the authorities thought it was just some tasteless prank.

"It turned out that the tapes were stolen from a local collector. Then Mr. and Mrs. Grath's house was broken into in St. Augustine, and a second set of tapes were discovered in Jacksonville, so a criminal investigation was launched. Plain-clothes police officers were posted in every Walmart in Savannah, Georgia, watching the canned goods sections. The third set of tapes appeared without anyone knowing how they got there. Security footage was scoured after the fact, but no one could be seen placing the tapes there. On top of that, some of the canned goods seemed to have disappeared.

"It was at this point that a more thorough investigation began in earnest. Petty thefts, mostly of food, were discovered all along the path from Orlando to Savannah, and more started popping up on the road to Columbia. Voice recognition software indicated that the voices on the tape were, in fact, those of the *Lorentz'* crew, or at least top-notch fakes.

"Still, the whole thing was treated as some elaborate ongoing prank until four mysterious car crashes took place near the end of May of that year. Four cars crashed as if they had hit something, denting the hoods, smashing the windshields. But the cars had hit nothing. Or at least, nothing visible.

"When the Richmond tapes indicated that four of the crew members had died after being hit by invisible forces, the scientific community began entertaining the idea that the crew of the *Lorentz* was somehow here on Earth, but unable to interact with the rest of us, except in a handful of random violent encounters.

"We still aren't sure how such a thing is even possible, but when two cars had similar crashes on the DC Beltway in rapid succession, then this final tape turned up, it seemed to confirm that there was more going on here than a mere prank, however elaborate.

"Tracking Major Novak's continued progress up the East Coast became difficult, as the disappearance of enough food to feed a single person is less noteworthy than the disappearance of food for seven or eight.

"Still, our research group at MIT discovered that a corner grocery near Major Novak's childhood home has had small, regular shortages over the past couple of months. We made a tape of our own that explained what we knew about what happened to Novak, and placed it next to the regularly disappearing food with Novak's name on it. For several days it just sat there, but yesterday, it disappeared. An hour ago, the tape was found where we had first placed it. This is the message we received."

"So you're saying I'm all alone here, and won't be able to find anyone else? Yeah, I'd kinda figured that out anyway. Good to have that confirmed though, I guess. And it's nice to know that not everyone's dead.
Tell my parents I love them, and miss them. Tell the rest of the crew's families I'm sorry."

"And that was it. Short and sweet. We plan on leaving another tape for her later today, asking her to work with us to understand what is going on. We will let her know that she should feel free to record personal messages, which we will pass along. In the meantime—"
"Professor, something just—"
"I'm right in the middle of a teleconference! We are making discoveries that overturn the way we understand the world! What could possibly be so—"
Whispered: "Something invisible just landed on a car stopped on the street in front of One Boston Place. It completely smashed the roof of the car. It appears to be about the size of a human body."
"Oh. Oh my. That means this tape was—Tell her parents—oh…"
The professor gulped.
"Friends and colleagues, I am afraid I have to cut this presentation short while we investigate a new, um, development.
"Goodbye."

Anya watched as the large sandbag appeared to explode, then hang in the air. Satisfied that this would stop them from contacting her again, she sat back and watched the sunset from the top of the tall building.

Now those assholes won't give my parents false hope. They can mourn and move on. Because the truth is, I'm already dead, or might as well be. I'm just not quite ready to be done living yet.

Tethered
by Megan Santucci

Megan lives in Southeast Ohio. She is a full-time mom to two extremely creative kids and a part-time content writer.

Celine was asleep when it happened, but the blaring of the master alarm had her unbuckled from her sleeping bag and halfway to the door before her brain even consciously registered that she was awake.

By the time she somersaulted into the cockpit, Peter was already at his station, his coverall over one arm as though he'd been teleported there in the middle of dressing.

"Talk to me," Celine said.

"We're not dead so that rules out about one thousand different scenarios," Peter replied, adjusting his foothold so he could type with both hands. "We're reading an impact on one of the ventral tiles. Venting water from the outer hull but the inner hull is holding so far."

As he spoke, Celine got her feet hooked onto the bar and pulled her own monitor towards herself to see the alerts unspooling across the screen. "Can we get a camera on that section? See what the damage is?"

"Working on it."

Sanjay and Sophie had both appeared and found their stations by the time he finished speaking.

"Sophie, raise Nairobi, update them on the situation," Celine said.

"On it."

Celine pulled up the clock app. Over the course of five months, they had cycled closer to and farther from Kenya time as the ship's rhythms trained them to follow a 24 hour and 37 minute clock. So for them it was the middle of the night, but for the people at Mission Control it was about 8:00 in the evening. She imagined the engineers eating dinner or watching TV or spending time with their families and suddenly having their phones blow up with messages.

"Got it," Peter said, then swiped at his screen to push the image onto the large central monitor.

"Fuck," Celine muttered under her breath.

The thing about reinforced carbon-carbon—the thing everyone *knew* about reinforced carbon-carbon—was that it was very, very good at resisting heat but very, very bad at resisting impacts. She had been a child when *Columbia* disintegrated over Texas, but she could still remember it in the way you remembered the monsters who lurked in your childhood closets. And of course she'd read about it since, studying it from every possible angle. And they'd run simulation after simulation where this sort of thing happened to the *Genesis*.

But that wasn't the same as looking at it. Looking at the bottom of her ship splintered like a slate smashed over an impertinent classmate's head. Looking at a crumpled section of plastic hull with a ragged gash running through it. Looking at water venting into space, boiling and freezing at the same time, ice crystals spilling across the black sky like a galaxy of newly formed stars.

It made her feel cold, to think that that breach in the hull was basically right under her feet—maybe thirty, forty meters away at most. Probably closer.

"Can you get footage of the impact?" Celine asked.

"I should be able to."

Earth was on nearly the opposite side of the sun from them right now, so it took 20 minutes to get a message there and 20 minutes to get a response. By the time they got their first comments from Nairobi they'd had the opportunity to watch the video of the incident dozens of times. A meteor roughly the size of a basketball had sped past the tail of the ship and skipped across the hull like a stone on water, leaving a trail of carbon fragments in its wake as it careened back off into space.

This was one of the million and one scenarios they'd anticipated, of course. The overwhelming majority of space debris was essentially dust, with maybe a grain of sand thrown in here and there for variety. But every now and then you had pebbles or even rocks. They'd just been unlucky enough to encounter one of the bigger rocks, out here in the vastness of interplanetary space where you didn't expect to run into anything.

Celine started handing out assignments after the first time she watched the video. Seal off and drain the section of hull below the breach. Get repair kits ready. Send out the bigger pieces of replacement material on the robotic arm. Make sure the EVA suits are ready to go.

So she was ready, several more painfully slow exchanges later, when Nairobi gave them the go-ahead to do what Celine had figured out hours ago—they would have to do an EVA.

The four of them crowded into the EVA prep room. Sophie helped Celine get changed and Peter helped Sanjay, but gender segregation was kind of an empty gesture in such close quarters. Plus, Sanjay was gay. Plus, if a straight man was moved to perverse thoughts at the sight of a 60-year-old woman in a sports bra and an adult diaper, more power to him.

The first layer was a cooling garment, which looked like long underwear with hoses running through it. It basically *was* long underwear with hoses running through it. The necessity of this garment tended to surprise the average non-astronaut, but contra Khan Noonien Singh, it was not necessarily very cold in space. The thing about space was that it was empty, so there were no molecules to excite with their body heat. So, it tended to linger around them. When they were doing hard physical labor and working up a sweat, it lingered even more. Hence the cooling garment.

Over that went the pressure suit. Unlike the classic inflatable suits, these maintained pressure via a network of tiny metal wires that coiled up when activated (Celine was pretty sure it was electromagnetic? Or something? But that wasn't her area of expertise.) so wearing one felt a little like trying to move around in a pair of skinny jeans that were a size too small. Not that Celine had ever tried that in her younger and more foolish days.

By the time they were fully suited up, Celine could already feel herself sweating under the cooling garment.

"You ready for this?" she asked Sanjay over the comms.

"Born ready," he said cheerfully, giving her a stiff thumbs up.

Celine returned the gesture. They pulled themselves into the airlock, waited through the depressurization cycle, and daisy-chained their way to the outside of the ship. From there it was a slow, easy float to the damaged panels, propelling themselves along via the handholds spaced every meter or so along the sleek hull of the ship.

No matter how many times Celine did this, it never got old. You wriggled your way out of the airlock like a chick hatching out of its egg and then pushed off slightly with one hand and turned around and there was just…eternity. Blackness deeper than the deepest darkness possible on Earth. And a million billion stars blazing so bright it seemed like you could reach out and touch them and burn your fingers.

Finally they reached the hull breach. It looked innocuously small up close, maybe half a meter across. But that small breach was spread across three different RCC panels. The first part of their job was to remove those panels and see what was happening to the plastic underneath.

Celine let herself float for a minute while she planned things out in her head. "Sanjay, I'm going to take handrail 1175 here. Can you go to..." She had to squint to read the numbering, which really seemed like a design flaw. "...Handrail 1124, and we can get this panel from both sides?"

"Copy that." Sanjay floated to the handrail she'd indicated and set up his tools.

The process of unscrewing the panels was tedious, especially here in space where everything was just different enough to be difficult. Celine's wrench kept sliding off the bolts and bouncing to the end of its tether like an overeager dog pulling the leash during a walk.

Celine decided she needed a distraction. She flipped onto a private channel so she could talk to Sanjay without all of it going into Mission Control logs.

"How's Chandra?" she asked by way of conversational opener.

"He's good," Sanjay said, his voice warming at the mention of his husband. "He keeps telling me about all the amazing food he's eating back in Houston, though, which is just rude if you ask me."

Celine chuckled. "I'd kill for takeout from Earth right now. What kind of places do you two like?"

"Well, Indian food, obviously. And in Texas there's a ton of Mexican places. Tacos and burritos and so forth might not be the first thing you think of when you're looking for vegetarian, but there are so many options it's honestly not difficult."

"Yeah, I could see that."

"What about you? What would you get if you could get anything delivered?"

Celine finally got the tricky bolt loose and gave a triumphant little laugh. Then: "Ugh, anything. Sushi. A burger. When I did astronaut training in Montréal, I lived down the street from a bagel shop, and I have literally had dreams about a proper Montréal bagel. We get plenty of bread, you know, but it's just…disappointing."

"I know exactly what you mean. On the chem team we have this whole conspiracy to just bake bread all day when we get to Mars and call it science."

"I mean, it's not like it's not science!"

Sanjay laughed. "Okay this end is ready to go; how are you doing?"

"Give me a minute."

It took several hours before they finished all the repairs. Celine was sweating and breathing hard, all her muscles aching, but she kept her voice upbeat when she said, "Okay, I think that's it. Let's pack up and go."

"Roger that," Sanjay replied.

Celine collected her tools, double-checking that she had everything, and then started rappelling her way back up the side of the ship.

In space, no one can hear your line snap, but Celine felt it. The force of the recoil sent her into a spin. Her back slammed against the side of the ship. Terror flooded her veins with adrenaline. And then some kind of training reflex must have kicked in because she found herself clinging for dear life to a handhold, her heart pounding so hard it felt like it might explode.

Sanjay swore.

"I'm okay, I've got a handhold," Celine said. She looked around to orient herself and noticed ice crystals floating off into the black. She hoped the snapped line hadn't cut another hole in the hull. That would be annoying.

Then she noticed that some of the ice crystals glinted red in the slanting sunlight.

She followed the trail of ice down to her leg and saw at once that the water was coming from her cooling garment. The red stuff was coming from a long, razor-straight gash along her thigh.

For a second she took this all in in a scientific sort of way. How interesting. That had never happened before.

Then the pain hit like someone had taken a blowtorch to her leg.

Celine bit back a scream and clung more tightly to her handhold. "Sanjay," she managed to gasp, "we have a problem."

"I see. I'm coming to get you. Just hang on."

"Hanging." Celine thumbed off her mic so she could swear loudly and colorfully.

"*Genesis*, we have a suit breach," Sanjay said as he crab walked across the hull, his voice dead calm. "Aborting EVA. Prep the airlock for emergency repressurization. And get Thad, tell him to stand by."

Thad was the ship's doctor.

"Celine, talk to me," Sophie said over the comm.

Celine thumbed her mic back on. "My tether snapped. Cut up my leg. Hurts like a motherfucker."

"Okay. Are you still in contact with the ship?"

"Yeah."

Sanjay came even with her, grabbed her free hand, and squeezed. "I've got you."

Celine squeezed back.

"We need to get back to the airlock. I can tow you, but it will be faster if you can help."

"Yeah."

Sanjay unclipped the end of his tether from his belt, threaded it through a carabiner, and then clipped the end to Celine's belt so she was now firmly attached to the ship.

"Okay, one hand after the other. Come on."

Celine crept beside him over the hull. The slightest jolt to her injured leg was agony. After a few meters her vision started to gray out and her grip on the handholds started to slip.

"I've got you," Sanjay said, his voice still dead calm. "Just a little farther. Stay with me."

Celine was a pilot. She was used to pushing past pain. Used to fighting off unconsciousness in dangerous situations. But right now it was all she could do to focus on Sanjay's voice as he towed her slowly towards the airlock.

The next thing she knew, there were hands supporting her from all sides. Someone took off her helmet and someone else strapped a plastic mask over her mouth and nose. Celine's vision cleared a little. She saw Thad take a very large pair of scissors to her EVA suit—that was going to be a bitch to replace—so he could peel it away from her injured leg.

It felt like he was ripping off her skin instead. Celine screamed and felt herself blacking out again.

"Mae, get me 5ccs of ketamine," Thad said.

Celine was aware of a stabbing pain in her good leg, and then slowly wasn't aware of anything else at all.

When Celine came back around, she was floating gently against the restraints in the single bed in their tiny sickbay. Thad was floating near the ceiling, scrubbing blood off a bulkhead. The perils of slicing yourself up in microgravity.

Thad turned around to see her looking at him. "Hello. How are you feeling?"

Celine took stock. "Still alive?"

Thad chuckled. "That's good. How's the leg?"

"Really sore."

"If it hurts worse just give a holler and Mae or I can get you more painkillers. You got a really nasty laceration, plus burns from, you know, being exposed to space minus a suit, so it'll take a while before you can get back to work."

Celine sighed. "Just hearing that makes me feel bored."

Thad chuckled again. "Remember, I'm used to dealing with injured pilots. And you're already tied down."

Celine grinned. "I'll listen to doctor's orders. I just won't like them."

"You don't have to."

It was the next morning, according to the clock, when Thad ushered in Peter.

"Now remember," he said, holding up one finger in warning, "I reserve the right to kick you out if you upset the patient."

"I'll be on my best behavior," Peter promised.

"So what's up?" Celine asked as soon as the paper-thin door closed behind Thad. (He'd be able to hear their whole conversation, but one maintained the illusion of privacy or one went mad.)

"My team did a thorough evaluation of the tether that snapped," Peter said. "And consulted with Nairobi. To make a long story short, the tether wasn't designed to withstand the temperature extremes involved in interplanetary travel so it corroded over time and that's what caused the accident. So the good news is it wasn't an error on your part."

"And the bad news is, it wasn't an error on my part," Celine replied. "If I'd fucked up I could do better next time.

But what are we supposed to do about tethers that aren't able to do the job we need them to do?"

"The official stance at Mission Control is that the tether failure is within the bounds of acceptable risk," Peter added, his tone making it clear what he thought of that assessment.

"The fuck it is," Celine replied heatedly. "And I'm not just talking about my own life here. If the tether had snapped an hour earlier and we hadn't been able to finish our repair? The whole crew would be at risk when we try to land."

Peter threw up his hands in frustrated agreement. Then he glanced at the corners of the room and Celine remembered suddenly that this was the only room on the whole ship without security cameras. Apparently all of the finalists for ship's doctor had put down their collective foot and insisted it would have been a slap in the face to doctor-patient confidentiality.

Peter still spoke in a low voice. "I've got the engineering team working the problem. I mean, they didn't *technically* tell us not to."

"You're worried," Celine said, more of a suggestion than a question.

"It's my job to worry," Peter replied. "You don't get to another planet by not having contingency plans." He sighed and ran a hand over his close-cropped hair. "And—look, I'm not saying Mission Control isn't looking out for us. I don't want you to think I'm saying that. But I think that if you'd died, the people up at the top at MCX would hand it off to a PR person and not lose a minute's sleep at night. It's not a people problem to them. It's a money problem and an image problem."

"This doesn't sound like something you just started worrying about yesterday," Celine said, watching him fidget like a man who wished badly to pace around.

"Oh, it's not. I grew up there, remember. I was there when MCX first moved in and took over a couple of villages like we were nothing. One person, thirty people, a hundred people...it's never mattered to them."

It wasn't the first time Celine had noticed that Peter was the only Kenyan on the *Genesis*. But it was the first time she'd had to look him in the eye while she was noticing it.

She looked away first.

"I don't want us to be like that," Peter said earnestly. "I don't want Mars to be like that."

There were a lot of things Celine could have said to that. A lifetime worth of things. But she just said, "Sounds like you have a lot of work to do."

He smiled a little. "Roger that, Captain."

Shortly after Peter left, Sanjay brought her breakfast and then hooked his feet to the floor and started on his own food.

"Hey," Celine said while her oatmeal packet heated up. "I just want to say thanks for yesterday. You kept your head and that probably saved my life."

Sanjay shrugged. "We're fifty million kilometers from other humans. If we can't count on each other, then..." He shrugged again. "As for keeping my head, let's just say I'm glad I was wearing a maximum absorbency garment."

Celine laughed. "Be that as it may," she said once she had finished laughing, "I'm glad you're on my team. And I owe you one."

Sanjay grinned. "Once we have takeout restaurants on Mars, you can buy me tacos."

Cyanic Symphony for the Glovebox
by Maxwell Gierke

Maxwell Gierke is a 16 year old writer from Oregon, Ohio. He found his love for writing any his high school, Toledo School for the Arts, where he is two years into a three year period of studying Creative Writing.

The cyan picked paint peels from the dashboard
like a sticker on paper
below the surface coat of color
there is a symphonic crowd calling my name

I am filled with an intense urge for exploration

No matter my shape or approach
I can't seem to close the glovebox
once I'm inside

The cheers of my paint covered fans
can't pierce the droning noise of the running engine
with a final pull the door clicks shut
leaving me to myself

I glide my hands around the walls
to find a light switch
a deep yellow light fills the space around me

Sharp turns throw my body around
I can sense the van pulling out of my driveway
I punch and scream at the thin plastic lock
holding me down on this horrific roller coaster

I crash into a shelf
breaking some of the precious china in my glovebox
the loud noise angers the vessel
it shakes and grimaces increasing its speed

I tumble around trying to find my footing
the floors and walls spin around and around
until a sudden moment
where no barrier seems to withhold me

I am floating in my glovebox
moving through the air like an Olympic swimmer
circling the walls until I drop to the floor
breaking the freshly waxed wood planks
and opening my eyes in my bed.

Singularity
by Leah McNaughton Lederman

Leah McNaughton Lederman has created two volumes of Café Macabre: A Collection of Horror Stories and Art by Women *(SourcePoint Press, 2019; 2021) and her own short story collection:* A Novel of Shorts: The Woman No One Sees *(2020). Her creative nonfiction has been published in* The River and South Review *and* Defenestration Mag, *and she was nominated for a Pushcart Prize for her essay "My Bleeding Heart" in the online anthology,* What is and What Will Be: Life in the Time of Covid. *Leah is active in several writing communities in the Midwest, where she lives with her husband and an assortment of children, cats, and dogs.*

She was still breathing.

She would expand into the space around her and she knew, from some atavistic pit within, that's what it was. Breathing.

She had to pin it down, shifting rusty gears inside of her, or it would be gone.

The next breath had to happen.

Inhale.

It was too much to hold. Her body would fall back into wherever it went when she was gone.

She was only awake when she was breathing.

Exhale.

The dreams were static noise punctuated by flashes of clarity, some unseen hand within her turning a radio dial.

A radio dial. A relic. Her grandmother had one she toyed with during summer visits.

Inhale.
How long had it been?
Exhale.
Was there more to remember?

The longer she focused on the breathing, the longer she could stay awake.

Inhale.
She gathered the fragments of her senses well enough to look around.

Exhale.
She was hovering in some sort of mesh made from…what was it? Beams of light? They crossed over her and under her and held her in place.

Inhale.
Everything else was dark.
Exhale.
There were others.

Sometimes the clicking sounds brought her out of the motionless limbo.

They came from outside of her; they came when she was breathing.

She heard the clicking and she saw the webs of light.
Inhale.
Click-k. Click-k. Click-k.
Exhale.
The clicks came in sets of two or three.
Click-k. Click-k.
Inhale.
Always a rhythm.

Exhale.

Inhale.

There had been a life inside of her, once. Voices broke through the hissing thrum of her dreams. Were they words? What are words? What—

Inhale.

She saw colors, though she no longer knew their names. When her mind flashed, she saw the bright ribbons and flowing fabric. The faces.

Exhale.

She worked to conjure the images in the dark behind her eyes. The dark there was different; it was her own.

Exhale.

Now she had the breath, the colors. The faces.

Inhale.

She saw them standing, first on one leg, then the other. Arms arced upwards, attempting grace. The children—

Exhale.

It had been a dance.

Click-k. Click-k.
Inhale.
Click-k. Click-k.
Exhale.
Next there will be three, she knows.
Click-k. Click-k. Click-k.
Inhale.

A separate rhythm came from inside of her. Colors, only soaring through the air. Music.

Click-k. Click-k.
Exhale.

When the second set of clicks scraped through her ears, she was ready.

Click-k. Click-k.

She moved a finger with each velar stop, in time with the sounds in her head.

The next inhale was a gasp. And then there was nothing.

It took her a long time to remember how to breathe again.

Inhale.

She wondered, as she breathed out—*exhale*—how many times she'd learned to breathe, to expand into the space around her. It seemed familiar. A dance she done before.

Exhale.

She was re-aware of the dark now. The breathing, the light, the colors, the faces. Aware that she'd known them before, and that they'd been taken from her.

Inhale.

There were no words, but she knew now that words were a thing that was missing.

Exhale.

The clicks came more often now.

CLICK-K-K-K. CLICK-K-K-K.

She inhaled sharply. They were louder now, closer…

They'd changed the rhythm.

Exhale.

The flailing arms on stage. Twirling, dizzy faces. Hands—*hands!*—clapping.

A new sound came from inside of her, high-pitched and familiar, warm: *Mommy!*

Another sound came from inside of her, but it melted into the outside of her and trailed down the thing that was her face.

Inhale Inhale Inhale
Exhale Exhale Exhale

Inhale Exhale Inhale Exhale
It was like choking, and she couldn't breathe.

She brushed the air with her fingers, then trailed her arms through it. The beams of light holding her shifted reluctantly against these movements. She did what the children had done in the dream from inside. She moved her arms in arabesque and remembered…

They were with her in the mirror, following her movements. They focused on their breathing.
CLICK-K-K-K! CLICK-K-K-K! CLICK-K-K-K!
Darkness.

Inhale.
Remember…
Exhale.
She felt weak. The light beams tethered her, held her suspended in the air, quivering with each breath she took.
Inhale.
Remember…
She watched the light beam bounce, slightly, as she twirled her finger.
Exhale.
The beat was coming from inside of her now. She hadn't heard the clicks for some time. They'd had a rhythm, she remembered.

The figure in the laser web nearest her shuddered. It had never done that before. She'd known that there were others, she'd been aware…but now they were moving, too.
Inhale.
Sometimes she heard them breathing. Gasps, sighs, sobs. Each breath she heard kept her awake, kept her alive.
Exhale.
She heard a laugh and she joined it.
Inhale.

Alive.
Exhale.
She saw another web quiver and she tapped her finger to make her own web quiver, too.

Heartwood
by Chris J. Bahnsen

Chris J. Bahnsen is an assistant editor with Narrative magazine. *His work has appeared in* The New York Times, Los Angeles Times, Smithsonian's Air & Space, Hobart, River Teeth, Hippocampus, *and elsewhere. In July of 2021, his short story "Octagon Girl" appeared in* Palm Springs Noir, *an anthology from Akashic Books. He divides his time between Southern California and Point Place, Ohio.*

Once the clockmaker's hand with extreme sensitivity winds the mainspring using a small brass key and the very first beats tick into the world, the mantel clock experiences a precise awakening in the small stone-floored workshop.

The clock sits on the workbench, noble, weighted, like a miniature palace of exquisite wood awaiting a miniature emperor. Through the open sash window, in the distance, a floodplain races toward an upheaval of mountains that break the sky, at the foot of which the mantel clock can fathom the Great Forest. The clock's wooden skin contracts with longing, though it does not yet understand why.

The old man's puffy face lowers to the clock, mustache swishing in time with the ticking heart. The melody from Haydn's oratorio Creation hums in his throat, and his eyes lavish the bezel's gleaming edge, how the cornice overhangs the main structure like an earnest brow, the way the pillars of Carrara marble on each side of the clock glow with pearly translucence.

The clockmaker feels a demanding heft rub his ankle. He bends over, straightening again with a well-fed orange cat splayed as if boneless across his arms. "Look, Cleo. Look what I've done this time." He floats the slack bundle nearer the clock. The cat extends a rosy nose and flexes her nostrils at it. He quickly pulls her back. "Not so fast my little savage! The varnish hasn't cured yet." To this she sneezes.

The old man carries Cleo to the open window. "Better for kitty if she takes fresh air," he says. The feline pours out of his arms onto a hedge-top below the window, somehow making herself weightless as she walks across it and jumps into the summer's eve.

Five chickens picking at the bare ground near their coop alert on Cleo and, clucking and flapping, dash for shelter. In an outbuilding just beyond, the pink blunt of a nose edges out of the shaded doorway. The nose seems to follow Cleo who swishes across the dirt yard, tail up high with a curl at the tip.

Godawful shrieking.

From the doorway an enormous pig charges, face puckered and twitching with rage. A single wiry eyebrow overhangs its beady glare. Less than a fortnight ago, the swine had snuck up behind the clockmaker's wife as she milked the goat and gave her a mauling about the ankle. She'd been nagging at him to butcher the pig ever since.

The legs though short and stumpy carry the pig with daunting speed. Cleo's regal poise humps in alarm and she races for the chicken coop. Her body compresses then springs straight upward with an ease remarkable for a feline of twenty-one years. Her front claws catch the edge of the coop's overhang, scoring the shingles as she yanks herself onto the roof.

At the edge of the overhang, seated with sphinx grandeur now, the cat regards her bawling subject below, ramming its head into the wall in frustration. From inside the coop, a squawking din. Wing claps of harried chickens. Feathers and straw dust belch through gaps in the planks. The pig throws its front hooves up onto the wall standing on its hind legs, only inches from Cleo's face. The cat's left forepaw disappears then returns to where it was, the only evidence of contact being the pig's snout, bloodied and flayed open now. The brute falls onto all fours, wailing and spinning, dragging its nose along the dirt to salve the pain.

"Such a mischief maker," chortles the old man, admiring Cleo from the window. "Getting spryer, I think." And he knows full well the reason, reflected in his own youthful gait as he returns to ogling his latest work.

In carving the mantel clock's housing, in fashioning and assembling the pallet cock, pendulum bob, the chime flirt, each delicate spring and mechanism, he has not only created another work of art, he has harnessed the life force of a most special wood. The clock's ticking energy will further sustain his aged heart, a heart that should have worn out some time ago. For in this clock he has used up the last of the heartwood, chopped from the ancient matriarch, towering oak of the Great Forest. And by doing so he has also ignored a bidding handed down along with the enchantments of woodcraft from his father and grandfather: *Never, ever, take an axe to the Mother Oak.*

A familiar heat of sadness blooms in his chest reminding him that, had Granddad and Papa done as he, perhaps they would still be here today.

"Bad hearts seem to curse your family, Ben," Doctor Maiwald told him on his last house call. Over eleven years ago. "I recommend you retire posthaste. No more axe swinging or moving heavy clocks about. Otherwise, may as well ride into town and order you a pine box from the Hesse brothers." That was the supposed healer's worthless prescription to the fainting spells, the heaviness of limb.

Ben lets out a *humph* of satisfaction. Here he is still alive and working, Dr. Maiwald long rotted in his own pine box.

Not long after the doctor's visit, Ben had found the branch on the ground near the foot of the Mother Oak, as if an offering from her, scorched by lightning but most of it salvageable, given the beauty, the rare grain of the wood. And then a noticeable return of vigor once he'd created the grandfather clock now standing near the doorway. So it was true. The sacred oak really did hold such power. Surely there'd been no harm done. And if a mere limb could do that, what would the heartwood do?

More time to work. To create magnificent time instruments, admired in manors of nobility and perhaps, one day, in the royal palace itself. That was all the old man craved. Now he could go on indefinitely, and his wife, unknowing to her, would gain the same longevity, as would anything in frequent nearness to the clocks—even the hobo spider bedding up in the east corner. Yes, his love for Bertha has been muted by the passing of years, but who else to see to his comforts?

The mantel clock flexes its big hand ever so slightly, feels a gust from the clockmaker as he lets out a sigh of contentment. When at last the old man pegs his work apron on his leave, the clock's skin contracts with longing again, for its wood, though rent from its original form, holds grains of memory from whence it came, of a roiling green canopy, the sensation of swaying, whistle of mountains dragging their teeth through the wind. Soon, up through the quiet, come ticking whispers of others in the room: the giant grandfather clock, a bell-strike skeleton clock and dome, the gold-finished grasshopper clock, a triple fusee eleven-bell musical bracket clock. And so many more. All of them orphaned children of the Mother Oak.

Their mechanistic murmurs tell stories of their common origin, of terror and violence, how they've been waiting for the mantel clock to awaken. But they are too rushed, ticking with the urgency of hard rain. The newborn is not yet able to grasp their language, their words. But it can at least sense their kinship.

Outside the window crickets rub their wings in chorus, and fireflies blink lemon pulses that blend with emerging stars.

The ticking murmurs quiet suddenly and the clock grows aware of a strong swishy heartbeat creeping below. What could that be? the clock wonders. As if in answer, an orange streak flames upward and past, four creamy paws landing on the workbench. Silken fur strokes the clock. It recognizes the creature from the day, though her eyes have dilated into crystals of strange ocher.

Whiskers tickle the clock's face. A sniffing nose strafes its cornice. With the old man gone, Cleo can investigate at her leisure. And by the feline's tender body strokes and the exquisite sound of purring, the clock knows friendship.

But the clock, in its infancy, has misunderstood.

Cleo is actually smearing it with her scent, claiming the clock as another of her subjects. Once that's done, she lifts a front paw and at the tip of each toe a sickle unfurls from its pouch. Cleo drags their needle-sharp tips across the clock's back plate, exactly where its skin is most vulnerable, unvarnished, and when she feels the wood open and bleed splinters, her purr changes to a *hiss* of satisfaction.

The mantel clock tries to scream from the pain, but it does not know how to break voice off the hour.

As she has taught the other clocks, so must the feline teach this one: it is not special. It must learn early on that *she* is the special one. The ruler of night. She is clever, this puss.

She leaves her mark behind the clock, where the old man won't readily notice. And she knows this wood is alive, can heal itself if given time. So she will repeat this lesson with frequency. She will be slow, most cruel, in teaching the newborn its place.

Having made her point, Cleo elongates to the floor and slinks toward the grandfather clock near the doorway. A moonbeam shimmers off its long wagging pendulum. The lofty clock presses its back into the wall trying to hide in the shadows. It does no good. Just before exiting Cleo bites into the lower corner of the grandfather's base so that the acid of her saliva enters the wood to fester. The timepiece lets out a dong of torment. The other clocks tick with arrhythmic fervor, trying more than ever to communicate with the mantel clock. But the newborn, wounded and terrorized, retreats deep within itself so it does not have to listen, hoping the old man with his gentle touch will soon return.

Just before daybreak, the clockmaker's wife comes into the workshop as if wading through market day in the town square, head bent forward like a battering ram, shoulders swinging, ready to knock anyone out of her path. Yet there is only her husband in the room, lit by oil lamps. He runs a soft cloth over the mantel clock's finish.

When the cloth first passed over its back panel, the clock anticipated great pain. But the pain did not come. And the old man has detected no scratches, for during the night the wood has healed. But the clock thinks the old man has cured its wounds.

A rooster crows with first light. Through the window, out in the mountain valley, the Great Forest is reborn in amber and gold.

Bertha stops short of her husband. The colors of her only housedress are washed out. Her spine crooked from toil.

A snort directs her gaze out the window. Near the outbuilding, the pig roots at clods of dung then flips on its back and rolls them flat, not a care in the world. Ben still hasn't slaughtered the horrid thing. Rides his cart mare all those miles to chop wood but can't step outside to butcher that stinking swine. They needed the sausages. Her eyes find his axe, hung on the wall beside the workbench, bloodless.

She inspects his work area.

"Ben, where is the crate? That clock should be packed by now."

The old man seems unaware of her presence. He opens the mantel clock's face lens, breathes on it then wipes the inside of the glass.

"Ben!" she repeats, stomping a foot, which sends a jounce through her dewlap.

Ben turns to her, removes his pince-nez and lets it suspend from a chain. "It likes being touched," he says. He aligns his spectacles back on his nose and goes on polishing every contour of the clock.

Bertha tries softening her voice. "Don't you see, dear? You must get paid for all your hard work. You mustn't get attached again."

The old man keeps polishing. Bertha's drawn-out sigh causes him to straighten and sweep his hand around the workshop where on all sides the heartwood clocks sit, stand, or hang from a wall, their ticking like murmurs of an impatient audience waiting for a show to begin. "The ones I keep are quite special," he says.

By now, Bertha has grown desensitized to the wonder of her husband's clocks. Except for one. It sits in the far corner on a stool. A carousel clock. Wood-carved horses with gold-plated saddles on galloping cranks. The platform completed a lap every minute then, on the sixtieth lap, the horses whinnied the number of each hour over carnival music. But the carousel no longer responded to a winding. She misses its company in the sitting room where she takes her morning tea before even the rooster awakes. Ben made the clock for her on their first wedding anniversary. She'd asked him to repair it months ago.

If only she'd known Ben would not be a good husband, that she would have to do other people's wash and farm chores, besides running her own household, so she could buy needful things. Wool clothing and blankets to survive the winters, feed for their dwindling livestock. And then if she was frugal long enough, perhaps the luxury of a new brazier or having the cobbler resole a pair of shoes.

She kneads her hands, laments their roughness. Wonders why she didn't leave him years ago, when her breasts were higher, before her flaxen hair had coarsened into a gray conundrum and she could still catch a gentleman's eye, one who could've taken care of her properly. But now, she attracts little more than blowflies.

"Ben," she says. Cleo appears at her feet, sits against her shin in solidarity. "You will send this clock to Mister Odenhausen where it belongs. He commissioned it and we need that money."

The old man shifts on his feet and shakes his head. "This isn't his clock," he says. "Mister Odenhausen was good enough to grant me more time on his order." Lovingly, he buffs the mantel clock with the cloth. "This one will stay with us."

Bertha's lips tremble with bitter sadness. Even if she'd been able to give him children, he would no doubt have favored his clocks over them.

The other clocks draw into unified meter.

Cleo jumps onto the workbench, pushes her muzzle under Ben's hand, forcing his attentions. "Yes yes," he says, abiding the cat with long strokes along her back, up her tail. "You can stay with us, too, pussycat."

His hands gather Cleo under her belly so that her body collapses, flaccid, as she's being lifted, legs dangled yet stiff, anticipating the gentle toss to the floor.

The mantel clock's secondhand adjusts its time. Ben lowers an ear to listen. "Notice how the beats have synchronized with the others?" he says. "I didn't do that, Bertha. It's the clock's doing...isn't it wonderful?"

When Ben smiles at his wife his mustache spreads like the wings of a white egret. Bertha does not smile back. The money she had counted on would be delayed now. She looks beyond him out the window, toward the little mountain village she came from. Would they remember her?

"All right, Ben," she says. Cleo hears an unfamiliar tone in Bertha's voice. For caution's sake, the cat wends out of the room.

"That's my girl," says the clockmaker. "You're too good to me." His cheerfulness burns her with disgust.

"Perhaps you could freshen my tea, dear?" her husband says. Not waiting for an answer, he shuffles to the other end of the bench for his teacup and saucer.

When he turns back Bertha is wielding his axe above her head, the heavy blade poised over the mantel clock. She wants him to see her hack it to smithereens. The cup and saucer slip from Ben's hand and clatter onto the bench. Carefully, so as not to spook his wife, he reaches for the axe, his voice a prayer: "No, Bertha...you would be taking a life. Let me help you understand."

The mantel clock ticks faster. It perceives the menace of the axe above and in that moment awakens to the native wisdom in the grains of its heartwood. In turn, it understands the metered chant from the others...*find...your...power...complete...our...power...*

Bertha relishes her husband's desperate attention. She can't remember the last time he kept his eyes on her this long. Their wedding night? Lust then, fear now. With a giddy cackle she brings the axe down.

"No!" Ben shouts as the blade whacks the roof of his precious mantel clock.

Sparks explode from the axe on impact.

The blade does not penetrate. It rebounds instead with equal and opposite energy, for the clock has petrified itself to a diamond's hardness. The blunt end of the blade knocks Bertha in the mouth, breaking off teeth, and when she cries out the air rushes over the exposed nerves jangling them raw.

The axe slips from her hands. Overwhelmed by the pain, she buckles over and dry heaves. Tooth splinters dribble from her mouth.

The old man, groaning in distress, closely examines the mantel clock for injury. First he listens. Yes, still ticking. He caresses the housing, inspecting it for structural cracks, indentations, grazing. But he finds not the slightest evidence of the immense blow.

Whimpering babble at his feet.

The very sound of it stirs a dark maelstrom in Ben's breast.

Bertha, on all fours, her mouth dripping blood, daintily plucks her tooth chips off the floor. "Ben, you can fix them…yes, you can fix my teeth," she snivels and turns her face up to him. The last thing she glimpses is the axe blade rushing down. The wet *thunk* of her hewn skull never reaches her ears.

Hands tight on the axe handle, the clockmaker stands over his crumpled wife, daring her to move. But her stare is infinite. "Mad old bitch," he snips, booting her rump for emphasis.

He examines the mantel clock once more, rechecks every centimeter. Remarkable, how there's no damage. Then he taps around the housing with his knuckles. "Hard as…why, you were defending yourself!"

The mantel clock utters a lyric chime as if in answer, pure as a songbird's first note after an April shower. Its sound exquisite, beyond the old man's original design. All the other heartwood clocks respond with a single ding, coo-coo, chirp, gong, knell, harp. Ticking applause rains down on the clockmaker.

Delighted, he turns to the center of the room, opens his arms as if to embrace his flock of timepieces. "You are all so very special," he invokes with tenderness, "each one of you loved as my own child."

A tear trails down a ruddy cheek into his mustache. He only wishes Poppa and Granddad could behold this glorious moment.

Soon, the applause disseminates into a smattering of ticks. The old man's smile decays and his ears perk when he realizes some of the clocks have stopped. As the quiet expands, his limbs grow heavier, so heavy he braces a forearm against the workbench to fight a sudden fainting spell, the weakness. A whumping pulse, like the blades of a giant ceiling fan turning slowly, fills in his head.

"How can this be?" he murmurs, knowing that he wound each clock on the first day of the week as always.

Squeals draw his gaze out the window.

The pig is bolting from the barn straight for Cleo, who runs toward the coop. But her legs are no longer spry and when she jumps cannot get her to the coop roof this time. She falls back to earth and the clockmaker cries out as the swine's mangle of teeth grab Cleo by the nape of the neck and shake her and bash her into the earth. Cleo's caterwauls are ungodly before she falls silent.

From inside the coop, chickens peek out in hushed fascination. Their small brains unable to comprehend the sight of Cleo, queen of the barnyard, limp in the pig's jaws now.

The clockmaker turns away in tears. His face levels on that of the mantel clock. Its ticking slows, then nothing.

Clinging to the workbench with all his fading strength, he thrusts a brass key into the clock's winder and twists it clockwise. But the mainspring won't take the wind. The clock remains silent like the others. By now it knows the old man is not its creator, but an enslaver who has profaned the Mother Oak, and it gleans impressions of what waits—broken sunlight through a ripple of leaves, roots thick as anacondas half-submerged in mossy earth, a sense of swaying in lofty space. Peace unending.

"Do not abandon me!" Ben pleads, watching as an emerald mist rises from the mantel clock's housing. He tries to scoop some of the vapor with his hand and mash it into his stuttering heart. Vines of mist bleed from the other heartwood clocks and converge into a phosphorescent cloud near the ceiling.

Sliding to the floor, the clockmaker wails against a silence that, without clock song, without the ticking chorus of mainsprings, enters his mind like black ice, and the lustrous cloud, complete now, drifts out the window into the morning clarity, tailing toward the Great Forest.

Turbulent Airspace
by Barry Burton

Barry lives in Columbus, Ohio. He writes in the wee hours of the morning, before going to work as a physical therapist. This is his first publication. You can reach him at @bbwritesstories.

When The Handsome Flyer appeared, Tom thought he was its latest victim. He couldn't deny that the name the news had given the thief was fitting, now that he was witnessing its work first-hand.

It was a custom-build, clean and silver, with sixteen copter blades and two pairs of modular wings. It looked like it belonged in the sky, the way it effortlessly cut through the air, changed directions on a dime, molded its shape to suit its function.

Tom's Beetle was boxy and orange, with more legs than copter blades. It looked like it hailed from an earlier and uglier era of drone manufacturing. It was the best he could do on a small fixed income, made smaller by recent medical bills. Initially he wasn't thrilled about its looks, but it was sturdy and the battery held up for the long hours he sent it out foraging for mushrooms. Its many legs allowed him to crawl over rugged terrain, and its hatchback provided ample storage. By setting up a payment plan, he was able to afford a pair of crude manipulators for handling the mushrooms he found.

The latest victim of The Handsome Flyer turned out to be a sleek black octocopter hauling a sack of groceries.

Tom was relieved but also a bit embarrassed for thinking the city's most notorious drone thief might bother with his Beetle.

The whole thing only took about ten seconds. The Handsome Flyer flew out of the trees behind the Shop How You Want store. Tom had the Beetle perched on the lip of one of the dumpsters. He was checking to see if anything good had been tossed out. The silver predator flew past and snagged its prey in a Faraday Net and turned back around, flying over again and towards the trees.

It was then that he remembered that the police were paying money for tips accompanied by a picture of The Handsome Flyer.

The Beetle's camera had just came into focus when the thief disappeared into the trees.

What could he do? It'd been a rotten week. He'd no luck finding Chanterelles, despite all the rain. His basement was flooded, despite new gutters. And now, because he had an old brain and a budget flyer, he'd missed out on some easy money.

He was about to go back to picking through the dumpsters when he heard branches snapping, deep into the trees.

Tom had the Beetle in the air, flying towards the commotion without a second thought. He wasn't the best flyer, so when he got to the trees, he swooped down to the ground and crawled at top speed.

Bits of Faraday Net glimmered like tinsel in the webwork of tree branches.

He crawled the Beetle past an onion, a bag of carrots, a busted stalk of celery.

Beyond the wreckage of groceries, he came upon the black octocopter, lodged upside down in a pit of mud. Its motors whirred helplessly, the copter blades churning mud, feet wriggling in the air.

He scanned the serial code on its belly and messaged its owner, one Vanessa Harsworth.

T: Hello. I saw what happened. I'm beside your rig.

V: arg! damned hb! what's my status?

T: You're flipped over in a mud pit, so I can't tell. HB?

Vanessa: handsome butthole. u mind getting me out?

T: Let me try.

Tom replaced the Beetle's crude manipulators to grip the octocopter's feet and scuttled backward. Her flyer was about twice the size of his own, and his manipulators were too weak to keep a grip on the flyer's legs as the Beetle pulled.

T: Having trouble getting you out.

Vanessa: what are u using?

He sent her the Beetle's specs. A hatch on the side of her flyer opened, slapping the mud.

V: use my spares

He switched out the crude manipulators for a pair of three-pronged grabbers made of titanium. The fingertips were coated in some kind of textured rubber material. With the grabbers, the Beetle had no trouble dragging the octocopter out of the mud pit and flipping it over.

T: You're out.

The octocopter's front was caked in mud. A layer sloughed off when it unfurled its own manipulators, the same three-pronged grabbers on the ends of two beefy telescoping arms.

V: now to get the dirt outta my eye

One of the grabbers pulled a towel from the storage hatch and wiped the mud from its camera. Bits of glass came off with cleaning.

V: still can't see anything. something lodged in there?

T: It's actually busted.

V: rats. send me a pic?

Tom sent a picture of the jagged hole in the camera lens.

V: grr thatll be a pricey repar

V: repair*

Vanessa turned the octocopter in a circle, then started the copter blades, throwing a ring of mud on the nearby trees.

T: Copter blades and legs look to be in working order.

V: thank fn god

T: No kidding.

V: ok ive got another favor to ask

T: Shoot.

Vanessa walked him through the steps to cast his Beetle's video feed to her computer. After that she had him climb the Beetle up on the octocopter's back and grip the sides with the three-prong grabbers.

V: ur a saint. i dont live far

The speed of the octocopter made the ride unlike anything Tom had ever experienced. It cut through the trees and soared on the wind over the city like an eagle.

T: My hip is giving me a little trouble. Mind if I take a minute to walk it out?

V: stretch that hip!

Tom eased himself off the couch and peeled off his controller gloves. He watched his TV screen for a few seconds to make sure the Beetle wasn't going anywhere. Then he gingerly stepped onto his bad leg, the one with the fractured hip, the plate and screws, and limped around the house. His physical therapist wouldn't have approved. He was supposed to get up every two hours, but the crappy foraging led to dumpster diving which led to the fiasco with The Handsome Flyer.

Handsome butthole.

She was a nice lady. He was glad to be of service.

Surprised really that he could be of any with such a shoddy rig. But it was better than nothing, a tool for mushroom foraging since he couldn't go "traipsing" anymore.

That's what the doctor had called it. No more traipsing he'd said. The fall and hip fracture happened at a park. A pair of smooching teenagers called for an ambulance. Three months later and it was still aching.

Tom walked back to the living room and found the TV screen completely green. He thought maybe it had gone nutty. He eased himself back onto the couch in front of the computer and scrolled through Vanessa's messages.

V: holfjyhb!
V: holymother of
V:
V: ughhhhhhhhhhhh
V: fml D:<
T: What happened?
V: the fricken hb happened
T: Why's my video feed green?
V: its called sticky ammo. we r covered in it
T: Can it be wiped off?
V: negative

Tom slipped on the controller gloves. The left was frozen stiff, like the fabric had been soaked and put in the freezer. The right had some resistance, but it moved.

T: I can move my right manipulator.
V: ok, got anything sharp?
T: Don't think so.
V: ok. i think we're screwed then
V: sorry for dragging you into this
V: never thought hb would come for me twice
V: mustv really pissed them off when I shredded the faraday net.

Tom almost said it wasn't a big deal. His Beetle wasn't worth much anyway. But the truth was the Beetle meant he could forage despite his bad hip. Without the Beetle there'd be no more of that, and with it no more birdwatching or leaf collecting, no more marking the seasons by the shift in colors, the entrance or departure of specific mushrooms and birds that signaled a change in weather. He'd be bored out of his mind.

He got up from the couch again and limped around the living room. His hip was throbbing like a bad toothache. Sometimes he wished he could just rip it off and get a new one.

When he returned to the couch, he got an idea.

T: Going to try something. In the meantime, do you mind reporting our location and heading to the police?

V: sure

The chances anyone would come in time weren't great, but they had to try. The police routinely told the public they hadn't the resources to enforce laws in the air. There were too many flyers and too much airspace to do any good. The best they could do is offer rewards for tips and bounties for apprehensions of lawbreaking drones and their operators.

He used the right manipulator to take hold of one of the Beetle's legs and pulled it off. He'd remembered the foot pads had little cleats on them. After a few minutes of scraping, he'd cleared enough of the lens to see The Handsome Flyer's silver underbelly and its arms gripping the octocoper's frame.

V: wha?? how'd you do that?!

Tom held the dismembered leg in front of the camera.

V: hahaha

Tom freed his left arm and pulled out another leg. Then he scrubbed the Beetle's copter blades. He got most of it off, but they still wouldn't move. He guessed the goo had seeped into the motor and seized it. So the Beetle would drop like an anvil if it slipped off the octocopter.

V: im streaming your heroics!

T: Don't tell me that. I'm no good under pressure.

V: ok im not streaming. no one will ever know about the brave little beetle...

T: I'm going to try to free your manipulators.

V: watch out for its gun

The octocopter's manipulators were folded into its chest, just under The Handsome Flyer's front eye and its gun. The end of the barrel was stained with remnants of sticky ammo.

Tom raised one of the Beetle's detached legs in view of the predator's eye. It panned down and the gun spat out a green gob, nearly knocking the limb from the Beetle's hand.

It would be impossible to avoid the gun while clearing away the sticky ammo from the octocopter's arms.

He scraped the goo from his rear hatch and took out a wad of mesh bags, what he stored his mushrooms in. He smooshed them down with the grabber, sizing up the gun's barrel.

Then he stuffed the manipulator into the gun barrel.

The gun fired and shook, squeezing Tom's hand as it jammed from its own goo.

Its operator threw The Handsome Flyer into multiple barrel rolls, trying to shake him off. The Beetle bounced on its silver underbelly. He lost the Beetle's liberated appendages and watched them shrink to nothing.

The jammed gun was the only thing holding him to the tumbling flyer.

V: yessssssss1

V: bwahahahahaaaa!

The Handsome Flyer tried a few more maneuvers, contracting the machine into a bullet-shape, dive-bombing for the ground, pulling up at the last second. It was useless. The Beetle and the gun were fused like Siamese twins.

Tom used his free hand to tear off another leg.

As he was scraping free the octocopter's manipulators, he received an anonymous chat request.

THF: GIVE UP TOM BERTMAN.

T: Why hello there!

THF: I KNOW WHERE YOU LIVE.

T: Would you like to come over for tea?

THF: RESISTANCE IS FUTILE.

T: I've heard that from somewhere...

The Handsome Flyer dove again, this time towards a long park with soccer fields at one end and a baseball diamond at the other.

Tom saw a game in progress on the baseball diamond.

THF: IF YOU DON'T RELEASE YOUR ARM IM GOING TO FLY INTO THOSE KIDS DOWN THERE

Tom brought Vanessa up to speed with the situation, which was getting way out of hand.

V: omg

V: they wouldn't

T: I think they might...

The Handsome Flyer swung low into the soccer fields, picking up speed and steamrolling the grass.

They say you're not supposed to negotiate with terrorists, but all that was at stake here were a couple flyers. Pretty banged up flyers. Sure, Tom didn't want this butthole to get his way, but the baseball players had nothing to do with this.

THF: LET GO!

T: Letting go.

Tom hit the manipulator's arm release and waited for the Beetle to tumble off and his screen to go black. It didn't budge. Something was stuck.

T: I can't let go! It's stuck!

THF: LIAR!

He told Vanessa he was stuck, his arm wouldn't release. He had the Beetle bashing the jammed arm, trying to break it loose.

V: give me control
T: How?

She sent him a link. He clicked it and it downloaded a file to his computer, freezing his screen for several seconds.

They were closing in on the outfield. Tom could see that the baseball players were children, about the age he'd discovered mushroom foraging. It was his sport, he'd told his parents.

He saw that the outfielders had noticed the big silver thing flying toward them, but they weren't moving out of the way. Why weren't they moving?

THF: THEIR BLOOD WILL BE ON YOUR HANDS

Tom: I'm telling you it's jammed! Pull up! I'll give you whatever you want!

Suddenly his controller gloves were moving on their own, like they were possessed. He felt his right hand tighten as the Beetle leveraged the fused manipulator to swing itself onto the front of The Handsome Flyer. His left hand balled into a fist and swung at the flyer's ugly black eye.

Glass debris twinkled and faded and then everything was tumbling.

Tumbling and tumbling.

Children were shrieking.

Tom's stomach leapt into his throat.

The feed went black.

#

Tom was sitting in his car, about to head to the park. Vanessa was too and she was much closer, only minutes away. His organs felt scrambled. Every time he started the engine he felt sick.

T: I should've given you control earlier.

V: dont start that. i wouldve never thought to canabalize my own flyer. that was slick

T: I don't feel slick.

That old adage of watched pots never boiling was certainly at play. He pulled himself out of the car and carried his computer to the porch. Then he limped around his yard, hardly traipsing but the doctor might disagree. The grass was overgrown but not to the point of neighbors calling a code violation on him. His nephew had been nice enough to swing by every few weeks and run the mower.

As he walked, his eyes naturally scanned the ground, looking for mushrooms. It was certainly more gratifying to look in person, smell the outdoors, feel the earth's curves under your feet.

His eyes fixed on something orange sitting in the mulch next to his air conditioner. How ironic it'd be to find Chanterelles in his own backyard while he'd struck out all week in the parks.

Ah, of course. Just a piece of trash. He bent over and snatched it up. He straightened, surprised. His hip usually complained when he did that.

He went back to check his computer.

V: pulling in...
V: omg
V: Tom.
V: TOM!
V: your beetle looks mostly fine
V: also, kids are fine
V: haha
V: shoulda started with that
V: hb in a million pieces
V: mine too
V: gonna take a long time to clean that up
V: id help but all that grass would kill me
V: alrdy feeling sniffly and i havent even left my car
V: ...
V: TOM
V: ARE YOU ALIVE?

The operator of The Handsome Flyer turned out to be a Russian bot that learned to fly watching adolescents. Most people weren't very satisfied with that discovery, including Tom and Vanessa, but it had its upside. The authorities were going to start policing airspace, as best as they could.

Weeks afterward, Tom was headed to Vanessa's apartment to drop off a small basket of Orange Chanterelles. He could've delivered them by Beetle, but he was trying to walk more to strengthen his legs. His physical therapist had fit him with a pair of trekking poles that made it safer to do some light traipsing. Something about foraging in-person had brought his luck back. Or perhaps there was a subconscious skill to looking for mushrooms that hadn't been at play with the Beetle.

He still used his flyer, which Vanessa had helped repair and upgrade, financed by the reward money they split. He often had it follow him in the parks, and he made use of it when the terrain was particularly rough.

Vanessa spent her half on a pair of high-sensitivity manipulators, similar to the ones doctors used to do remote surgeries. Her allergies were so bad she rarely went outside, and the new manipulators greatly expanded the range of activities her flyer could do for her. Things like dealing cards in the bridge club at the local senior center and helping her mother change out lightbulbs.

She had insisted he give her nothing for helping him put his Beetle back together. She offered to give him flying lessons as well, free of charge. Her kindness had reawakened something inside him he'd lost after his fall, the months of debility and debt he wasn't sure he'd recover from.

And here he was, walking up to her porch. In person.

The Chanterelles weren't payment. They were the highest form of compliment, one Tom reserved for the best humans who happened upon his humble patch of airspace.

Comfortably Numb
by Tom Barlow

> *Tom Barlow is an Ohio Writer whose works straddle the literary, crime, science fiction and poetry markets.* Over 100 may be found in anthologies including Best American Mystery Stories 2013, Best New Writing 2011, *and* They Said, *and many periodicals including* Hobart, Temenos, Redivider, The Intergalactic Medicine Show, Crossed Genres, Mystery Weekly, Red Room, *and* Switchblade. *He is the author of the science fiction novel* I'll Meet You Yesterday *and the crime novel* Blood of the Poppy.

The smug look on the high school counselor's face told Dayne Oakes everything he needed to know about the results of his graduation placement exam. As the class clown, Dayne had become all too familiar with detention meds to mistake the counselor's smile for compassion.

"You scored 15 points higher last year, on the practice test," the man said, bringing Dayne's academic test results for the past 16 years onto his holo screen. The line trended ever downward. "I can't believe you people treat a test that determines your future like it was a pop quiz."

Dayne, still hungover, refused to meet his eyes. Sure, he should have skipped the baseball team's end-of-season party the night before, but his family had a long history of choosing short-term gratification over long-term benefits.

The counselor said, "Anyway, I'm sure it'll come as no surprise that you're being warehoused." He reached into his desk drawer and brought out a transparent package of capsules, all but one of them small and pink, the last large and purple. "Here's your first pack of warehouse meds. As of now, you're off the Juvicalm. Take one of the 10 mg. Psyrene daily. The purple one is Voyd. That's for emergencies, should you have an allergic reaction to social meds. Understand?"

While Dayne's dad had plateaued at 250 mg of Psyerene daily, his mom, showing small signs of dissatisfaction, had just progressed to adding daily doses of Euforia, the last rung on the complacency ladder. Now Dayne was expected to start down that same road. Sure, most of his friends were being similarly slotted, no big deal, most of them felt, as more than half of the U.S. population was warehoused.

But he and his twin sister Claire, embarrassed by how their parents embraced their worthless lives, had made a pact to better themselves, despite the lack of encouragement at home. The benefactors who held the relatively few jobs necessary in the highly mechanized society looked down on those who did nothing to earn their existence, and many times they had heard their parents disparagingly referred to as ballast. Now he had earned the same moniker.

"How'd Claire do?" he said, dreading the answer.

Sure enough, the counselor said, "She's the class valedictorian. I gave her starter packs of Concentr8 and Retayne, for university." She and Dayne had experimented with both drugs years earlier, only to find the nanobots in their blood that blocked opiates also refused to unlock these chemicals, recognizing neither of them were yet of age.

"You're as smart as she is," the counselor said as he closed Dayne's file. "You should be ashamed."

Dayne picked up his meds and stomped out of the office. While he was not short on self-esteem, thanks to

Juvicalm, he was forced to now face the reality that he would not be continuing his education, that he had nothing now to look forward to except a life of diversions and pity from his sister.

As usual, his parents were at the community pool when he arrived home. The Kitchen had already delivered dinner, more eggplant goop and white lab meat with tabbouleh. He hated parsley. He hated eggplant. And he longed for meat with a little texture; lab meat was about as chewy as the calfree butterscotch pudding that had been included with every dinner since he once foolishly expressed fondness for it six years earlier.

He was munching on the wedges of pita, the only edible part of the meal, when his phone alerted him that his best friend, Mohammad Abdi, was seeking a vid chat. Mo was the smartest person Dayne knew, and he'd hung with him through high school partly in hopes some of that would rub off on him. He thought briefly about rejecting the request, but figured he owed Mo a last conversation before his friend headed off to university and left him numb and dumb.

He expected to find Mo with a sympathetic look on his face, so he couldn't make sense immediately of the scowl. With the Placyd in the water supply, one didn't encounter scowls too often. "Hey, Mo. What's wrong?"

"How'd you do today?"

Dayne could feel the blush rising in his cheeks. "Crapped out. I never should have gone to that party last night. What was I thinking? How'd you do?"

"I forgot to leave my phone in the locker," he said. "I had it in my backpack, and when one of my moms called halfway through the exam, the proctor figured I was cheating."

The news astonished Dayne. Mo was the most conscientious person he knew, the last he would have guessed would make such a horrible mistake. Tagging him as one of the warehoused would be a tragic waste. With the burgeoning population, the race to synthesize protein efficiently was just one of many challenges that even ballast could recognize as crucial. Mo was the kind of person who could help solve those problems.

"That supremely sucks," Dayne said. "There must be a way to challenge that, isn't there?"

"If you're a child of a benefactor, you get a second shot at the tests. But my parents are both ballast. So, no, I'm screwed. I'm supposed to spend the rest of my life playing golf or cards, doped to the gills so I don't feel unhappy enough to cause trouble."

"Well, we can finally finish *Assault on Andromeda*," Dayne said, trying to cheer him up. "And look on the bright side—no more homework."

"I couldn't care less about holo games right now. And I loved homework. I love work. The way I look at it, a man without work might as well be dead. As my best bud, I wanted you to understand, OK? That way, you can explain it to the moms." Mo threw the feed from the security camera in his garage onto the screen of Dayne's phone, revealing Mo atop a chair in his garage, a rope around his neck. Before Dayne could scream, his friend kicked the chair over. As he watched in horror, Mo thrashed a few times before going slack, his neck canted to one side.

Dayne frantically phoned Mo's parents. One of his mothers answered. Dayne told her what was happening, but by the time she reached their garage, it was too late.

Even through the Placyd and Psyrene, Dayne could feel the pain at the loss of his best friend. He was aware that Mo had been cheeking his Juvicalm and evaporating his own drinking water for more than a year, claiming the meds clouded his thinking, but he never would have predicted the lack of mood meds would permit his friend to consider killing himself.

If Dayne wasn't so doped up, he might have cried.

His mother, Alejandra, found him moping on the back deck that evening. She had lived a couple of years of adulthood before Psyrene was available and was therefore likely to understand the way he was feeling, so he told her what had happened.

She took a seat next to him and grabbed his hand. "I'm so sorry your friend is gone. Perhaps we should have the Kitchen send over a dose of Amnesium 24-Hour; it helped me deal with the death of your granddad."

Dayne shrugged off her hand. "Mo wouldn't have wanted that. He believed in a clear mind."

"You know, those people in the Clear Mind movement?" she said. "They kill themselves all the time. You're so much better off following the Program. What's wrong with living a happy life? Maybe it's time I taught you bridge. Or we could go on a bicycle vacation. Would you like that?"

Even through the pain, Dayne found himself attracted to the idea of a vacation. This in turn peeved him; through the fog in his head one thought kept reoccurring; he should be mourning the loss of his friend more.

Dayne made it through the weekend thanks to the meds, and the efforts of his mother to distract him: bowling, Frisbee golf, parasailing with the family who lived next-door, binge-watching *Days of Our Lives*.

However, on Monday morning, when for the past 16 years he'd headed off to school, he felt at loose ends, even more so when Claire waved goodbye on her way to university. Alejandra suggested he accompany her to yoga class, but even through the drugs he was feeling a funk that he perversely felt like nurturing.

He was in the backyard reclined on a chaise longue, listening to the yardbot trim the honeysuckle bushes, when he heard his name called.

To his surprise, there stood Mo's older sister, Safiya, who had convinced Mo to go Clear Mind. Although she aspired to become a doctor and thereby a benefactor, she had started down that track a year ago without the aid of intellectual meds, which Mo had thought admirable or foolish, depending on the day.

Dayne found Safiya hard to figure out. For no reason he could identify, she had always treated him with familiarity, not afraid to joke with him, sometimes a little coarsely. She intrigued him, not the least for her reputation as one free with her favors, who went through boyfriends like other girls her age went through shoes.

"Hey," he said, scrambling to his feet. "How are you? Thought you'd be at school."

"I'm two weeks ahead on my studies," she said. "Can we talk?" She took a seat at the patio table. "I heard you were watching Mo when he did the deed."

He wondered if the transition from Juvicalm to Psyrene was doing something to his hormones; he knew the former had a reputation for dampening the libido. He'd always thought Safiya pretty, but that observation seemed deepened now. She wore her hair about as long as the bristles on a toothbrush, showing a lovely oval head, with a pair of button ears, a nose that was unapologetic and dimples that flashed whenever she smiled, which was not the case at the moment. Her complexion, the color of a trombone, was unblemished.

"You missing your brother?" he said, seating himself in the chair next to her. Up close, he could see her bloodshot eyes.

"Is it that obvious? You knew how close we were, right?"

He nodded, although Mo had underplayed this at school, worried that her notoriety would extend to him.

His modest reaction seemed to strike her wrong. "You're on the adult meds now, aren't you?"

"Starters. Low dosage. Why? Is something wrong with that?"

She pursed her lips. "My parents are way up the ladder with their meds, and it's driving me crazy the way they act like nothing happened. I put pics of Mo all over the house, but they react to them as if they were photos of an old hover they traded in. I thought maybe you'd feel something, but now I see you're already numbed up."

"I miss him," Dayne protested, feeling guilty that he didn't, more. "He was my best bud."

"I was hoping you could console me, but you don't even know what you feel, not with all that shit in your system."

"I can console you," he said, wondering just what exactly that meant. Looking to cover up his confusion, he said, "What's it like? Going Clear Mind?"

"It's lonely," she said, reaching across the table to take his hand. "There's hardly anybody worth talking to, except others who are clear. My moms want me to start taking Rdor, but I refuse to fall in love with the first schmuck that walks through the door. They figure once I'm married I'll quit rebelling. Yet they both have to take massive doses of Psyrene daily just so they can tolerate each other. When was the last time you were clear?"

"I have no idea," Dayne said, wishing that she was taking Rdor right now. The Psyrene was accentuating the pleasure he felt in her presence. "I think the parents put me on Hussh when I was four weeks old."

"There's a Clear Mind meeting at Happy Joe's Coffee Shop tomorrow. You should come."

"With you?" Dayne said, more interested in the company than the topic.

She squeezed his hand. "As my guest."

"Why me? If I'm so numb."

"You were Mo's best bud. Hanging with you is as close as I can get to bringing him back."

While going Clear Mind was not illegal, Dayne knew that attending a meeting would worry his parents, who were enthusiastic participants in the warehousing program. After lunch the next day, he grabbed his board and told Alejandra he was bound for the skate park. He was relieved to discover the Psyrene did nothing to inhibit his ability to lie.

Safiya was waiting, as promised, at the statue to Klaus Schmiegel, inventor of Prozac, in front of the Department of Health, which he found ironic. He noted that someone had glued devil horns onto Schmiegel's forehead.

The coffee shop was three blocks away. As they walked in that direction, Safiya said, "Now, you should expect to have some trouble focusing on what the speaker is saying; your meds are designed to shorten your attention span and zone out negative thoughts. You've got to fight through the fog. Luckily, you're on a pediatric dose, so there's still hope."

The idea that he needed hope made him a little uneasy. Was his family hopeless?

A dozen people were already in the community room when they arrived at Happy Joe's. As Safiya led him to a couple of open chairs in the circle, she explained that half of those in attendance were, like him, curious, the other half hosts who were already clear.

The group was looking to a light-skinned black man who could have passed for forty if he had dyed his white hair and the bushy fantail mustache. To start the program, the man introduced himself as Clarence Bishop, proudly told them that he had been clear for almost 20 years, since warehousing meds were first introduced. He then launched into a speech explaining the movement, which quickly lost Dayne. Or perhaps it was the presence of Safiya next to him, their knees touching with the tight spacing of the chairs. From time to time, she shifted her attention from the speaker to him, giving him a small smile and the flick of an eyebrow. Each time, a ripple of desire raced through him, far stronger than those he'd experienced while still on Juvicalm.

When question and answer time came, he asked the speaker how the process of going clear worked. The man nodded. "Good question. The answer is simple. Don't drink the water, don't take the pills. When you go in for your annual physical, refuse the booster shot. Keep a dose of Voyd handy should you accidentally ingest a warehouse med. When you became an adult at 18, you gained the freedom to do that."

Another girl about his age said, "There must be a downside, right?"

"Of course. The downside is you'll see life the way it really is. When bad things happen, you'll suffer emotional pain. The first 30 days are the most challenging; after that, you'll calm down. If you're like most of us, about then you'll come to realize how boring the usual distractions are; I've never played a round of golf, or taken part in a game show, or gone to a church service. With a clear mind you'll have to dig deeper to amuse yourself. But the good news is you can handle more intellectually satisfying pastimes. The warehousing meds make something like ethnology too difficult, but I've found it fascinating."

"Are you a benefactor?" another older woman said, accusation in her voice.

"No, and that's the key message here. You don't need to be a benefactor to live life as it actually presents itself. The powers that be think we need to be sheltered from ourselves, that merely making us happy will leave us content. I believe there is the ability in every warehoused person to deal with the burden of free time by digging deep into our true potentials. Failing your achievement test doesn't mean you can't lead a life of the mind; it shouldn't limit you to an empty life of the body."

A woman in her 40s with heavy facial tattoos raised her hand. "You don't take meds, but you accept federal food, a place to live, medical care, even the clothes on your back. So how can you criticize the warehoused?"

Bishop held up his hands. "Point taken. But I'm not criticizing anyone; I'm simply saying that, for me, this is a better life path. As for accepting necessities from the government, you know the meaning of ballast? Most people think it means dead weight, but in reality, it's the crucial mass necessary to keep a ship from capsizing. So when somebody calls you ballast, just say 'You're welcome.'"

When the audience ran out of questions, Bishop said, "If you decide to go clear, you might find it very lonely. Reach out to other clears, come to our meetings, make friends who share your interests. The pain is worth it, for the most part. It just takes a little courage."

On the way home, Dayne said, "So Mo wasn't brave enough? I think that's what I heard Bishop say."

"On the contrary; he was brave enough to decide when to end his own life. That's a right we all hold dear."

Dayne, seeing the sudden sadness on Safiya's face, quickly changed the subject. "Bishop repeated what you said about being lonely. How do you deal with that?"

Safiya hooked her arm in his. "You have to reach out to others, rather than wait for them to come to you. You want to come to our place? The moms left for a golfing vacation in Alabama this morning, so they could forget Mo. We'll have the place to ourselves."

"Are you sure?" he said, unable to believe his good luck.

"Why not?" she said. "We can console each other. If you know what I mean."

Dayne didn't, not exactly, but he was eager to find out.

\#

Afterward, sprawled with Safiya on her parents' king-sized bed, the window open to allow a delicious summer breeze to cool them, he said, "So why me?"

"Have you ever looked in a mirror? Now that you're off the kiddie meds, you're going to be overwhelmed by girls your age. You stay numb and you're going to end up married to the first girl smart enough to slip some Rdor into your cola."

He brushed his fingers across her cheek. "If I go clear, what about us?"

"We can try it out. But I'll warn you; you'll see the real me. For better or worse."

"I can live with that."

He began that evening at home by taking the dose of Voyd he'd been given when he received his new meds. Within half an hour he found himself crying without restraint, the loss of Mo like a knife wound. He desperately wanted to have a chat with Safiya, but it seemed somehow important that he find composure by himself.

Alejandra must have heard his sobbing, because she tapped on his door before coming in without invitation. "What's wrong, baby?" she said, brow furrowed.

"I'm going clear," he said.

"Oh, Dayne," she said, taking a seat on his bed. "Why would you do that? Is your life really so bad?"

He expected more distress on her face, but then realized how foolish that was. He'd never seen Alejandra cry, not once, even when she'd caught his father in bed with the blonde next door. "It's a way to honor Mo. He didn't believe in warehouse meds, and the least I can do is try to see the world the way he did, for once. I can always go back."

"Ten years ago, your cousin Elias went clear on a dare. A week later, he beat a boy half to death for asking his girlfriend to dance. He ended up on prison meds for five years. I don't want that happening to you."

Dayne was so awash with emotions he struggled to focus on her words. A little anger that she would challenge his decision, some filial love, fear that her warning might have substance, excitement at the thought of meeting Safiya on her own terms. "Trust me," he finally said. "You raised me to think for myself."

"We did? If so, it was by accident. I remember nothing but misery about growing up clear."

"You weren't clear. You had Prozac," he pointed out.

"No comparison. Prozac just kept me from being too sad. Today's meds make me happy. And you want to give them up?"

"My decision, Mom. You've got one child on the way to becoming a benefactor. Just write me off as a loser."

"You know I can't do that, baby," Alejandra said, rubbing him on the shoulder. "The meds won't let me."

He didn't know what to expect when he met Safiya the next day, as she suggested, at the library. She was waiting at one of the tables surrounded by shelves of what books remained in the warehouse section, mostly picture books and graphic novels.

She greeted him with a quick kiss, but this time, the shiver down his spine he'd experienced the day before was muted. She caught his look of puzzlement and asked what was wrong. He explained.

"That's the meds," she said. "Psyrene contains a bit of Orgazmia to encourage the warehoused to have frequent sex. They figure that takes the edge off of any residual angst."

"So I give up the excitement of sex?" he said. "And that's a good thing?"

"It's different. When you're clear you can enjoy the uncertainty. Will he or won't he? The chase has its own appeal. You don't have to work too hard to get ballast into bed."

"So yesterday you were taking advantage of my meds?"

"We start fresh today. How do you feel?"

"I'm overwhelmed with emotions, frankly."

"Let me show you something." She shoved a book lying on the table toward him. *To Kill a Mockingbird*. He picked up the book and gave her a quizzical glance when he saw the "Benefactor" tag on its spine. "What's this?"

"I took it out for you. Read it. You'll find you have the concentration now to follow along, and it might just speak to you. Let yourself respond emotionally to the story."

He picked up the book. So strange, to see a printed page. Other than the family Bible and some children's books handed down in his family for generations, he hadn't handled paper books much over the years.

"Bring it along home," she said, "and you can read while I do my homework."

"Your parents still gone?"

"Yeah, but that doesn't matter. They'd be happy to see me with anybody. They worry I spend too much time by myself."

While Safiya worked her way through a biochemistry v-class that afternoon, Dayne read the first quarter of Mockingbird. He was amazed at the way his emotions veered all over the map in response to the actions in the novel, between charmed and concerned, fearful and relieved. He wasn't sure he liked the agitation that seemed to come with clarity, but occasionally he looked up to catch a smile from Safiya. He also came to understand what she said about the hunt, wondering all through the afternoon if they were going to make love again.

Dayne woke after the first few days with Safiya with a vague sense that something dire was in the wind but was unable to pin it to any particular circumstance. Perhaps it was his dreams; they'd become so much more chaotic since he went clear.

He was beginning to understand that the emotions haunting him were disorderly not, as he'd expected, simply logical reactions to the ebbs and flows of his life. He tried to read more of *Mockingbird* that morning but quit after the tenth mood change inspired by actions in the book. After Kitchen delivered lunch, he phoned Safiya to see if she wanted to accompany him to a Clear Mind meeting, but she begged off, blaming a paper due in her arti-intel class.

He decided to go anyway. Bishop was running the meeting, and there were some new faces among the ones he'd seen before. During the question and answer session, he asked how they dealt with emotions that seemed inappropriate to the situation.

Bishop gave him a condescending smile. "Many people go clear expecting that they will turn into a computer, with each input tied to a specific output. You have to remember you're flesh, not silicon. There is in fact a source for each emotion you feel, but it may not be immediately obvious. Looking within, learning to understand yourself, is a lifelong project worthy of your efforts. You woke up blue this morning? Start there. What in your life could account for that? Often it's not something that actually happened, but something we fear might happen."

After the meeting adjourned, coffee and doughnuts were served to encourage those in attendance to stick around and chat. Dayne was about to duck out a side door when a young man in a wheelchair grabbed him by his shirt tail. "You want to know what's troubling you? I have an idea."

He introduced himself as Petr Diamond. "I was where you are a year ago," he said as Dayne took a seat so he wouldn't loom over the man.

"You mean, newly clear?"

"More than that. I saw you the other day with Safiya. Back then, I was dating her."

"She never mentioned you. Was it serious?"

He laughed bitterly. "I thought so. But the more time we spent together, the more I fell for her, and I found myself tied up in a knot for worry that she'd drop me. I'm not the best in the sack, thanks to," he poked his legs.

"You're not together now, so what happened?"

Petr made a spitting motion. "She's a head case. You wait and you'll see. Your blues are well founded."

"How so?"

"She gets her kicks breaking in the newly clear. I'm not the first, and you won't be the last she toys with. You reach an even keel and you'll be of no more interest to her. She feeds on raw emotions. Cry in front of her a few times and see how much that pleases her."

Dayne rose to his feet. "That's not the Safiya I know. You think you can pay her back for dropping you by ruining what she and I have? That's not going to work, pal." Before the man could respond, Dayne walked out.

The unfamiliar anger stayed with him the rest of the day, unrelenting as Safiya begged off that evening to finish her paper.

Dayne chewed over Petr's words for the next week as he spent as much time with Safiya as she would allow. She remained enthusiastic in bed but ruined the post-coital bliss by demanding he share his new experiences, in detail. He told her about how he'd yelled at his sister when she dared question his decision to go clear, about how much he resented the way Alejandra had cajoled her minister to talk to him about his rash decision, about how he cried and cried when he learned the neighbor's cat had died. How impatient he had become with Bishop and his meetings, how much he longed for her every morning after she left for school. How he wore his phone to bed in the off-chance she wanted to share some pillow talk.

All to which she initially reacted with rapt attention, like he was spoon feeding a meal to a famished man.

But in his life routine, things didn't change all that much, and, as Bishop had suggested, he was gradually reacting less passionately to the familiar. He could tell Safiya wanted more drama, and his life offered little real drama. In fact, he reasoned, the whole purpose behind the warehouse meds was to eliminate drama. He tried crafting a lie to please her, telling her about the progress of ALS in a cousin that didn't exist, and the fear he felt for him, but she saw right through his fiction.

Within another week, without the simple distractions that Psyrene made so attractive, he had little to look forward to in his life but her, and he suspected she was growing bored with him. She encouraged him to find intellectual interests, as Bishop had, but he tried book after book, vid after vid, and gradually had to admit to himself that he was no intellectual, meds or not. And as his addiction to her grew, she complained that schoolwork was making it difficult to find free time for him, that she was too tired, in a bad mood, beholden to her mothers. He gradually came to suspect that Petr had told the truth. But he didn't want to end up like him, bitter and lonely. As far as he could see, he had only two recourses, and he didn't want to return to the warehouse meds as long as he and Safiya had a chance.

He made sure to order the Rdor from the Kitchen so that delivery would take place while everyone else was out of the house. Fortunately, he and Safiya were to meet for lunch that afternoon in the smoothie bar on the nearby campus of her university. He arrived early and grabbed a table next to the window. He felt out of place surrounded by benefactors in the making, all carrying their 3D tablets and the occasional bound paper books, all with their noses buried in the same.

Safiya was almost a half-hour late. When he saw her coming up the street, he went to the counter machine and ordered her favorite green concoction, a blend of flavors not found in nature. The taste was strong enough that he was sure she would never detect the Rdor powder he mixed in.

When she took a seat next to him, he couldn't help but catch a whiff of a musk on her skin that was all too familiar. Nonetheless, there was no hint of guilt in her manner. As she sipped her smoothie she told him about the dissection lab that morning. He tried to steer the conversation to their relationship, but she dodged every segue with more biochemistry talk. He did note, however, that her hands were in constant motion, scratching her chin, stroking her tablet, drumming on the tabletop.

In an attempt to slow her down, he reached out and placed his hand over one of hers. She immediately withdrew it as though he'd dropped it on a hot grill.

"What's the matter?" he said.

"You moron," she said. She reached into her backpack and brought out a small pill box. "You know what happens when you've been clear for a long time? You get really sensitive to warehouse meds. You really thought you could pull one over on me? There's an obvious difference between real attraction and Rdor." She opened the pill box and took out a large violet pill that Dayne recognized as Voyd. "I was going to tell you we were through, but this just makes it easier." She took the pill, dry.

He sat, dumbstruck at his stupidity, despairing. "But I love you. And I mean really, no drugs involved."

"No you don't," Safiya said. "Nobody knows what real love is anymore. You might love the sex, maybe the illusion that another person finds you the most important person in the world. But you know what, Dayne? You're just another mediocre guy, one of billions and billions without any purpose to his life. You think you're brave? You couldn't go a day without glomming onto me. So no, you're not brave, not in the clear sense." She opened the pill box again and took out two other pills, one an orange and blue capsule, the other the familiar Psyrene. "Hold out your hand."

He did so, reluctantly, and she dropped the meds in his palm. "What's that?" he said, pointing to the orange and blue pill.

"Amnesium 30-day. Think of it as my way of letting you down easy. I've learned to not leave bitter boyfriends around to talk dirt about me."

"But I don't want to forget you," Dayne said.

She punched him lightly on the shoulder. "You've had enough of reality. You're the kind of guy that will love being warehoused. Take your meds. Be happy. And thanks for the ride."

She grabbed his wrist and raised his hand to his mouth. Dayne, unable to deal with the pain of loss that was overwhelming him, took the pills, washed them down with his smoothie. Safiya nodded, kissed him on the cheek and left.

Within fifteen minutes he was trying to figure out why he was in the smoothie shop and not at school. Not that he disliked the place. It had a comfortable atmosphere, and there were a couple of cute girls at the next table who were glancing his way from time to time.

He'd have to ask Mo about the memory loss. His friend was a genius; he could figure out anything.

In the meantime, life seemed damned good.

The Places Between
by Jacob Minasian

Jacob Minasian received his MFA from Saint Mary's College of California, where he was the 2016 Academy of American Poets University and College Poetry Prize winner. He is the author of the chapbook American Lit *(Finishing Line Press), and his work has appeared in publications including* Poets.org, Museum of Americana, RipRap Literary Journal, *and* Fire and Rain: Ecopoetry *of California by Scarlett Tanager Books, among others. Originally from California, he currently lives with his wife and daughter in Cincinnati, Ohio, where he teaches at Cincinnati State.*

"We can't stay there for long," Jackson said, splintering more than two hours of silence.

Marlene stared at him from the passenger seat. "You say that every time, Jackie. Every time."

Jackson gave her a quick peripheral look. Not an angry look. Not a pleasant one.

"Jesus, you'd think I've been in a coma these past four years," Marlene said.

"Has it been four years already?" Jackson's tone requested no response.

"Fuck you, Jackie. It just stresses me out is all." Marlene grabbed at the manual window handle, cranked the glass down halfway.

"Yeah," was Jackson's only reply. After a few minutes listening to the empty country air fill the car, "You think I like to be the one checking up on this fucking shit all the time, Leenie? You think I wanted to leave Nevada? Shit, it was the best thing we had going since West Virginia. But someone has to listen. Someone has to be responsible. Speaking of which..." Jackson hit the knob on the radio.

Static was all that sounded.

"Nothing," Jackson said. "What I wouldn't give for a fucking iPod right now. A damn cassette tape would do."

"Let's just go back to the deafening silence," Marlene said. "At least until we find some damn aspirin."

"Sounds perfect," Jackson said, "next to a full tank of gas, air conditioning, and a cold beer."

Marlene snorted.

Jackson gave her a stilted glance. "Or maybe a drive back through California."

"Stop the car." Marlene didn't move.

"Leenie..."

"Pull the car over right now, Jackie. I mean it. Right now."

Jackson slowed the '84 Mazda on the desert-fried highway, until the car and its attached storage trailer rested on the shoulder. Marlene snapped the door open and took a few quick steps away before stopping. She could already feel the asphalt's heat beneath the worn rubber of her Pumas. The sun had just passed its apex in the sky over the arid landscape, and she stared out at the sun-bleached brown of the dirt, the horizon's desolate undulations, empty save for a few dead tree trunks and branches, collapsed and weathered. She looked down and swiped at a tear she felt on her face before it had registered in her heart.

She hadn't heard Jackson open his car door when he stepped next to her, facing out toward the landscape.

"I'm sorry," he said. "Bad joke."

He looked at her, looked back to the horizon. They stood in silence for just over a minute. She was grateful for that silence.

Jackson continued, "I just...I think I just thought we'd have more time in Nevada. The ocean, the beach. We haven't been to a place like that in a long time." His chin lowered. "It made me forget."

She was aware of how much he loved it there. The beach where they had camped had the faint resemblance to a tropical island, waves calm across the grain. Jackson swam in those waves every day. But she didn't. She couldn't. All she could think about was what had drowned in all that water.

"C'mon," Jackson said. "The ARWS last said that we should be well into Minnesota by sunrise tomorrow." He looked up toward the sun's position. "We have to go."

Marlene turned and guided herself slowly back to the car.

"Got it!" Jackson said from behind the counter of the abandoned Shell station. "Pump Three. Let's hope it works. Remember to fill all the empties."

"I know," Marlene said, indignant, a tone that could cut diamond.

She considered making a snarky comment about his experience as a Chevron clerk finally coming in handy, but passed on the idea. No time for that now. They should have still been on the highway, headed toward Minneapolis, but a standing gas station was too much fortune to just pass by. The store's roof had been split open, the char marks indicating it was probably by lightning, but the tanks appeared to be intact, and the shelves looked as if they hadn't been completely ransacked. She picked up a can of three-cheese ravioli that had rolled under one of the broken refrigeration units.

"There's some good stuff here," she said, dropping the can into her backpack. "I can't believe we found this place."

Jackson stuffed a few rolls of toilet paper into his pack as he walked out of the bathroom. "You're telling me. But we have to be quick about...Oh, hey..." He appeared at the end of the aisle, an accordion of condoms unfolding from his upheld hand, bungeeing a few inches from the floor. "You sure we have to keep using these?"

"Yes," Marlene said. *Especially during all this*, she thought.

Jackson briefly looked wounded, and placed the condoms in one of the pack's zippered pockets. He disappeared from the aisle, but his voice carried through the store. "You should head out there now and get the gas going. I can finish the run-through of the store."

"Okay," Marlene said.

She began working her way back toward the entrance, but stopped at the end of one of the aisles. She reached her hand toward a shelf, withdrew it slightly, reached again and grabbed two boxes of pregnancy tests, shoving them into her backpack before exiting the store.

An hour after they left the gas station, the first signal of wind spoke itself into their minds. An hour after that, Jackson could feel it tugging at the unlit headlights.

They both bunkered in a knowing silence, the shared awareness that they may have run too far behind schedule.

"What does that sign say?" Jackson said, his voice heavy with the strain to dilute panic.

Marlene saw the highway sign, fallen from its metal post, leaning against the side of an overpass. All she could read was part of what she assumed was *Minneapolis*. The mileage was covered by either dirt or a large dark score from lightning; she couldn't discern which.

Rain began striking the windshield.

"I don't know. I don't know. All I saw was *Minneapolis*." She did not reciprocate Jackson's effort to hide panic. "Shit, Jackson, what are we going to do? Can you go any faster?"

Jackson looked down at the speedometer. "We're going one hundred miles per hour in a '84 Mazda pulling a trailer it's not meant to pull. Any faster and we could burn the engine out. Then we'd really be done."

"Are you sure?" She knew her question was superfluous.

"No. I'm not sure. Calculated risks, Leenie. Calculated risks."

They heard the first distant rumble of thunder. The rain became quicker and heavier, large drops drumming glass, roof, and hood. The sky was a darkening gray.

"Shit, it's rolling in quick!" Jackson said. "And we have no fucking idea how close we are!"

Marlene turned around in her seat, looking out the back window, her eyes large and teeth bared. Lightning forked the ground behind them in shorter and shorter intervals, splicing the sky with light. The thunder now became fantastical warlike booms that seemed to threaten splitting open the atmosphere.

"Marlene, turn around and put your seat belt on!"

"It's getting closer!" she said.

"Turn around! It's better if you don't watch."

The car began to shake with each fracture of thunder. Jackson could feel the wheel pulling hard to the left in his hands. He wrestled to keep the tires straight.

"Oh, shit!" Marlene said, turned back, and grabbed frantically for her seatbelt.

In the rearview, Jackson saw the trailer lift off the ground. A moment later, the Mazda's back tires lifted from the highway. He braced himself, his hands turning white on the wheel.

With a loud metallic twang, the trailer tore from the car, and was gone.

The rear tires of the Mazda landed back on the highway with a wet squeal. Eyes the size of cue balls, every muscle visible in his jaw, Jackson once again struggled with the steering. The back tires slid, causing a fishtail that could easily worsen to a spin. The car slowed to sixty, fifty, forty miles per hour.

The tires gripped the road and the car's wagging surrendered to Jackson's control. He kicked into the gas pedal and the speedometer needle climbed clockwise.

The lightning started striking the ground in front of them now, to their left and right, all around them.

"We lost the trailer!" Marlene said.

"Let's worry about that later," Jackson said. "We didn't lose us yet."

"That's everything we just lost!"

All their supplies, food, spare gas. Gone. And there was no guarantee they would be able to find any resources in Minneapolis. Just days earlier, Minneapolis was being ravaged by storms similar to the one chasing their Mazda now, similar to all the storms currently roaming the earth. The last calculation reported that over 78% of Earth was compromised by some type of natural disaster at all times. There was no telling which area would be next, which area would be clear, or what would be left after the storms had passed. The Automated Radio Weather System was the only warning they had, the only way they knew which locations would be safe, and the routes to get to them. And now, with California and the majority of the east coast under water due to rising sea levels, there were less places to go.

"We didn't lose *us* yet," Jackson repeated, low, almost a whisper.

Just as he brought the Mazda across the 100 mph threshold, Marlene pointed ahead. "Look, Jackson!"

Jackson could see it too. Ahead, a break in the sky, the gray ending into a pure gold-lined blue. Just miles away.

"I see it. I see it, Leenie."

A bolt of lightning hammered the ground just a few yards to the right of the front fender. The shock rattled their skeletons.

"Shit, that was close!" Marlene said, shaking the daze from her head.

"We're almost there. Hang on, Leenie."

Lightning strikes continued to pummel the earth around them. The blue in the distance grew wider and brighter. The pedal under Jackson's foot touched the floor of the car.

The back tires were losing their grip again. Jackson pressed the pedal hard into the floor.

"Hang on, Leenie!"

Marlene grabbed his hand as the rear tires lifted from the ground and gravity evaporated into weightlessness.

Four Poems
by Joshua Gage

Mermaid as Lover: A Definition

(accus.)	Her name is the rock upon which the ship of my heart shatters.
(antiq.)	The prayer of lovers made to Atargatis in the form of coital moans.
(arith.)	She plus the sea equals one. She plus the sea plus me equals one.
(astro.)	The moon, low and ripe on the horizon, swells the tides
(botan.)	The strands of seaweed in the sand, marking the indentation where her body blesses the shore. The wrack that binds my heart.
(catech.)	Why are my tears so briny? They remember the taste of her kiss and fall to seduce her out of the waves.
(conchol.)	Every shell she adorns her body with hides the name of a former lover.

	So many necklaces,
	so many combs in her hair.
(culin.)	The thin crust of sea salt
	glazing her nipple.
(eccles.)	Her body is the temple
	where I confess my sins.
	Each flick of my tongue
	ignites another candle
	until the building burns,
	and we are renewed by fire.
(ichth.)	Each scale on her tail is a ruby
	plucked from the crown of Poseidon.
(mus.)	The orchestral sound of waves
	exploding as she improvises a fervid aria.
(navig.)	I memorize the constellations
	of her body with my breath, learning
	the ways in which they tremble,
	driving me off course until I'm wrecked
	on her curves and drown.
(transl.)	A little death mourned
	by sea foam and luminescence.
(ult.)	The soft splash as she dives
	back into the water. The wistful
	aroma of coconut and ginger
	which lingers on my skin.
(voy.)	The dip of my oars in the water
	each night as her memory pulls me
	farther and farther from shore.

Venus Reborn

Attend all those who worship Beauty. Listen
to these waves and watch their waters shine.
Their foamy crests catch the sunlight, glisten,
then break, erupting with a flesh divine.
Emerald jewels caress her sacred curves
which shimmer in the ocean's morning mist.
We bow our heads, preparing to subserve
to Aphrodite's immortal holiness.
A lonely sailor, I long to navigate
the freckled constellations of her skin,
the gentle undulations of her tides.
I'll worship at her temple, supplicate
myself before her altar til twilight dims,
her statues dance, and the goddess is satisfied.

Ghazal

Behind my eyelids, my dreams are plagued by nightmares.
Even my red-eyed consciousness cries nightmares.

The goblin market wreaks of smoke and sweat.
Entrenched in shadows, the incubus buys nightmares.

The naked witches careen around their fire
as their unholy choir deifies nightmares.

The nun keeps watch over the sleeping orphans.
She thumbs her rosary against nearby nightmares.

The baby spasms beneath the ritual blade.
From out the moon's celestial maw fly nightmares.

The Pilgrim has visions of fangs and burning flesh
as into his sleep with echoing hooves ride nightmares.

Ghazal

Beneath her blanket, the young girl whimpers at the faces in the darkness.
She can hear them drooling in their secret places in the darkness.

The captain tends the wheel and navigates forgotten constellations.
He cannot sleep for fear of tentacled embraces in the darkness.

After vespers, the weathered monk shuffles to the scriptorium.
He slits his fingers to mark the codices on the bookcases in the darkness.

The witch will wed the rope maker's son, and he will teach her how to dance.
She spits an oily curse and climbs the scaffold's staircase in the darkness.

The Pilgrim shudders as his candles gutter out to tendrils of smoke.
He whispers cold prayers against the nightmares, but knows his place is in the darkness.

Take me to your Lowenbrau
by John Bukowski

John's background is medical writing, and he has penned a myriad of consumer publications, including website content, handbooks, and radio scripts. Several of his short stories have also been published. He is from the Midwest, spending most of his life in Michigan and Ohio, but is currently retired to eastern Tennessee where he lives with his wife and a dysfunctional dog named Alfie.

Bart pounded the bar and shook his head. He'd put up with a lot from his friend, but this was the limit.

"You've got to be kidding! Tell me you're kidding."

"I'm just saying," Pete said, "it has never happened, so we don't know."

"What do you mean we don't know? Of course, we *know*. Anybody in his right mind *knows*."

"There's no need to raise your voice," Pete said. "You're entitled to your opinion, and I'm entitled to mine."

"But your opinion doesn't make any logical sense. I'm beginning to think the monotony of the assembly line has monotonized your brain."

"Pardon me for not having a glamorous job like grocery clerk."

Bart pointed a cautionary finger. "That's food service specialist." He tapped the oak for emphasis. "*Senior* food service specialist, and second-shift assistant manager, thank you."

"You guys want another round?" Sam the bartender asked.

Bart nodded and waved toward the nearly empty glasses. "Let me get this straight. You're telling me that Batman could take down Superman. *Superman*? Is that what you're telling me?"

Pete Wysocki finished the dregs in his mug, then burped. "No, I am saying that they never fought, so we don't know."

"He's frickin' *Superman*, for God's sake."

Those were the last words Bartolomeo Garibaldi spoke before it happened. He wanted to say more, but his mouth went numb as a drilled tooth. He wanted to reach up to see if his face was still there, but his hand wouldn't move. At first, he thought he was having a stroke, but if so, Pete was too. Bart saw a blank stare in his friend's glazed eyes, drool and a few drops of Miller dripping from the corner of Pete's mouth.

There was no sound, which was the eeriest part of all. The low-level drone of the ballgame and the occasional traffic beeps were gone, as if he'd been suddenly sealed in plastic. The air felt thick as pudding and smelled like the metallic tang that comes after a lightning strike. Something was going to happen. Then it did.

First his glass and then Pete's began to shake, skittering across the bar like waterbugs. Pete's mug skidded off the side, but there was no clatter of breaking glass. The bottles lined neatly behind the bar joined the party, vaulting up and down like boozy Rockettes. A fifth of Heaven Hill headed to the floor, followed by some vodka. There was no crash and no pungent smell of booze, just that same metallic tang. Bart's ears hurt with the sharp, needling ache he sometimes got on planes. He wanted to hold them against the pain and overpressure, but his hands still refused to move.

Just when he thought his eardrums would burst, the glassware ceased dancing and reality came back with a rifle-shot bang. The mirror over the bar cracked, sending a shard of silvered glass into the oaken surface only inches from his hand. The ozone smell got stronger and a flashbulb pop caused his eyes to snap shut, the image of the barroom still burnt into the closed lids.

The electric stink departed, replaced by the familiar smell of old tobacco smoke and booze. Background noise returned, with the announcer saying that the score was three to two in favor of the Reds. Then a foreign voice, one not on the television, added, "Sorry about that."

Bart could move again. He opened his eyes and turned to see a funny little man dressed in what looked like a leisure suit made of quilted toilet paper. He seemed oddly human, although his askew hair was a strange shade of red, and his face held a glossy sheen that accented pale, almost translucent skin stretched taut around two beady eyes. "That's the inducer," he added, holding up a small silver box. "It always assures a grand entrance." His smile was pleasant, reminding Bart of his first-grade teacher.

"I'm Hamilcar Troska," he continued. "But you can call me Ham." Sniffing the air, Ham touched the little box and squinted in thought. "Hmm, simple ethanol molecules with traces of yeast, fusil oil, and various congeners." Ham looked expectantly at Sam behind the bar. "You drink it?"

Sam nodded dumbly.

"Fascinating," Ham said.

Bart found he could speak again, although his jaw muscles tingled and ached, as if he'd just suffered through a lengthy root canal. "Who are you?"

Ham chuckled. "You probably figured out that I don't come from around here." He pointed at the ceiling, twirling his finger before jabbing at the overhead light. "I come from the third planet circling a star right about there. We call it—

ah, never mind; you wouldn't know it. But anyhow, we have learned to utilize inverse-warp, matter-energy induction as a form of instantaneous travel. Well, not quite instantaneous." Tapping the box, he said, "This last jaunt was actually quite long: 4.3 milliseconds."

Bart, Pete, and Sam stared at the little man as he looked curiously around the tavern, grinning harmlessly. Two weeks earlier, in this very bar, the three of them had directed their considerable alcoholic and cinematic experience to this very problem. Bart had opted for kicking alien butt and letting God sort 'em out, ala *War of the Worlds*. Pete had voted for the gentler and more cerebral approach of *Close Encounters*. Sam had asked if they wanted another round, as in *The Lost Weekend*. But when barroom fantasy became miraculous reality, all reacted to the terrifying truth of alien visitation by simultaneously saying, "Can I buy you a drink?"

Ham seemed confused, but then his becoming grin broadened. Pointing to a bottle, he said, "You mean the alcohol?"

Bart nodded.

"That is a very kind and attractive offer, but I'm not supposed to. It might interfere with my medication. Although I haven't had any today, so it might be okay. What do you think?"

Bart gave Pete a 'what-the-hell' look. Pete stared blankly back. Both men turned to Sam, who shrugged. Then they all looked back at the odd little humanoid.

"Are you sick?" Bart asked.

The little man's grin never wavered. "That's a matter of opinion. Certainly, my doctors would say so, but I *feel* fine."

"What's supposed to be wrong with you?" Pete asked.

Troska's face bore down, deep in thought, trying to decide. He punched the little box and muttered, "Usually the translation function is quite good, but every once in a while…" Punching the box again, he shook his head. "No, that's not it." Another tap and his face brightened. "That's closer." A third tap and he said, "Yes, either of those will do." Looking up amiably, he said, "I am what *you* would call a psy-cho-path," he spoke the word deliberately, "or serial killer. It's a bit confusing in that both seem to apply." He tapped the box a fourth time and Bart couldn't move, only watch. Watch the strange little man with his strange little grin, the same grin Ted Bundy must have had just before a killing blow.

The little man reached into the pocket of his paper smock, removing a metal tube about the size of a Chap-stick. "I'd love to keep chatting, but they are going to find out I'm gone in a bit, so we have to hurry things up."

A menacing light shone from the top of the small metallic tube. Bart could hear it hum and smelled something like burnt wiring as Ham approached.

"Don't worry, the inducer will keep you immobilized so I won't mar your corpse. But I'm afraid the pain is going to be exquisitely intense, delightfully prolonged."

His disarming smile widened as he went to work.

Community of Me
by Scott D. Peterson

Scott Peterson is originally from Toledo, Ohio and has lived there most his life. As he grows older, he has learned to appreciate Toledo's creative community by performing improve comedy both through Glass City Improv and with his group named Downstairs Improv. He is a recent graduate from the University of Toledo English and Writing Studies master's program. He teaches Honors and AP English at a local high school.

I have forgotten who I am.

This, of course, is embarrassing for any shapeshifting species. To add insult to injury, I am trapped in the community bathroom of my apartment building. Shifting to the right appearance is crucial because wearing the wrong identity would cause suspicion from my neighbors. This is humiliating.

"Excuse me! You have been running that shower for the past three hours!" the Landlord continues as he knocks on the locked bathroom door. "I'm worried you might be flooding the room. Could you please turn off the water and come out now?"

My heart rate picks up speed as if I'm starting to run a marathon. My hands shake as the water continues to pour down my face. I need to change my appearance immediately, but I can't do that without first calming down. The process of changing requires endless amounts of focus. I will be exposed to the human world and mocked by my kind if I don't pull it together. I can see it now; many will tell stories about me at community gatherings. They will ask, "Did you hear about him?" and, "I heard he was exposed in a bathroom." I can already hear the laughs from those who I am forced to compare myself to.

This situation is not new to me. Rather it has happened on four separate occasions, three of which were within the last year. This has given me doubts in my abilities. I used to be able to keep my stories straight. Damnit, there were days where I was ballsy enough to change midday to another life and proceed with their activities. I wouldn't dare do that now. There are just too many complicated narratives for each persona. Now I keep it to only 6 different identities. That way I can be someone else each day of the week while giving myself a day to revert to my default form. It is important to remember that my life, though filled with different personas, is still my own. That underneath all of these details is a singular man, but who is he? What does he look like?

I turn around so that my face feels the pressure of the shower's massage function directly on my forehead. Each hit from the pulsating shower distorts my Saturday identity named Nick Howell. The muscles on my face lose tension and relax. My face droops down which gives it an almost inhuman quality. It is nice for a mere moment to let go of control and have an outside force dictate my appearance. My nose crawls from its high arched position to my lower right cheek. As the structure travels down my face, I can feel each muscle relax, create tension, and react to the moving feature. As it reaches an increasingly inhuman placement, I grab the nose and drag it back to the center of my face. I can still feel the plasticity of my body, but the years of wear and tear have made me nervous.

I push up on my cheeks to recreate the high bone structure that Nick, my pretty boy persona, seems to find so useful. I then poke each side of my face to create a slight indentation, which plants the seeds for dimples that even Shirley Temple would be jealous of. Lastly, I mold the accented arch out of my nose and give it the firm foundation this face relies on. I then attempt to hold this appearance for as long as I can.

The muscles on my face twitch and shake underneath my face. Each muscle, ligament, and tendon crawl as if they have a mind of its own until it gives out and droops to an almost unrecognizable form. I used to be able to hold personas for long periods of time but now I am lucky to get a day in each life. Any longer would ask too much of these aging muscles. I am exhausted but not tired enough to give up on all of my lives. Changing my appearance every day not only gives me some variety but allows me to relax some facial muscles and stretch out others. In theory, it should strengthen my ability and allow me to stay in one life longer. In practice, it forces me to realize my limitations.

The knocking grows louder on the door. It is as if there is a fire in the hallway and the only way out is through this particular bathroom. I quickly move to gather my things. I sidestep within the small quarters of this singular shower. I plant my feet on the wet tile and fall into the wall. The right side of my face becomes flattened. My nose, once again, moves across my face. I place it back in its rightful spot. I let out a sigh and compose myself.

"Everything alright in there?" asks the Landlord. "Do I need to call someone for help?"

"No! Don't call anyone!" I said. "I will be out in just a minute."

"Alright, can I ask who's in there?" said the Landlord.
Who am I?

A simple question. I ask myself this each morning as part of a daily routine, and my answer changes with the rising sun. I am the physical embodiment of a lifetime of lies, but I am also so much more than that. I am Nick, Liam, Damian, Salazaar, Lucas, and Amar. These six men make up a portion of me, but their lives have become too complicated, too hard to take care of. I feel like a single parent as they try to account for all their children's extracurricular activities. All of the dates, names, jobs, interests, and achievements have clouded over my default self.

Remember who you are.

I repeat this many times as the warm water attempts to relax me. Recalling basic facts about myself could lead me to self-discovery. My mouth lets out aimless rambles as my mind chases after my elusive identity. I am me. I am a Sculptor. A cute, albeit somewhat oversimplified term for my existence. Many would refer to me as a Shapeshifter, which is a stereotype that I will dismiss. Just because I can change my appearance, doesn't make me one of them. What a modern Shapeshifter fails to understand is that speaking in evolutionary terms, our community was here first. The Shapeshifters wouldn't be able to achieve their feats if my kind didn't achieve ours. Nevertheless, we are a dying breed living in a world populated with a more contemporary changeling. I tell myself I am not bitter, but who am I trying to fool? Evolution plays a cruel game.

"Umm did you not hear me? I asked who's in there?" said the Landlord.

I ignore the question and reach from the shower to grab the towel that was placed on the rack. I rub my scalp until there is no more water but notice that the pressure of the rubbing has given me unwanted signs of aging. I feel my face and notice wrinkles have etched themselves all over it. The crow's feet scratch out towards my cheek as the space below my eyes sinks like wet clay. By my guess, my appearance has aged nearly 20 years since I fell in the shower.

It is times like this that I envy shapeshifters. Those who can immediately and perfectly alter their appearance. I will never wish to be one of them but their abilities must come in handy in times of crisis. Meanwhile, I am left forming and sculpting my daily appearance. I am like a work of art. I can't be rushed.

Stay focused.

Who is that faceless persona? This is hopeless. I am pathetic but stubborn. Unlike a typical Shapeshifter who dons their appearances like a kid on Halloween, I lose myself in a role much like the latest Oscar winning actor. I can remember who I am underneath, but it feels as if someone else is in control. I take on more than just their appearance, I accept their personality, experiences, and even their aspirations. I think I am that person when I put on their appearance. That is until my body informs me through aching muscles that it is tired of holding this image which tells me it is time to change. This pulls me out of the personality and back to my default. This immersive trait, which is out of my control, helps me sell my identity. Each life is unique and challenging but still has much to offer.

My facial muscles are tense, partly due to the situation but also the years of extending myself too far. I stretch these muscles by first squinting as if I am trying to squeeze my body through a straw. I then open my mouth as wide as possible as if I am yelling from the top of a mountain waiting to hear the echo. I do this on repeat without making a sound. As I do this, I notice the straining and reluctance of my facial muscles. Once again, fears creep into my mind. Is my body telling me that I have become too old to keep up this charade?

I massage my cheeks to prep for a sculpt. My muscles are not used to performing under pressure, but I don't see many other options. I feel the stress and friction of my physique. I fear that they have begun to harden, which can happen when a Sculptor reaches old age. Eventually, my muscles will keep one constant form, and I will lose my changing ability. I spend a lifetime sculpting every day until my body decides it has had enough and changes its strategy. I am at war with myself in a way. My body could make this choice today, tomorrow, or even 20 years from now.

The Sculptor community considers those who can't remember part of their elderly community. Growing old as a Sculptor is like performing in many theatrical productions until you settle into the one role you were always meant to play. Of course, you're not the casting director. You don't get to choose the role. Rather you simply fall into the life of one of your personas and forget the others.

A pleasant thought, getting lost in oneself. Living a normal life. Others would see these thoughts as blasphemous. To that, I would say, so what if I am a heretic? I am also tired of keeping track of my lost self in a community of other personas. That is why Sculptors rarely reveal themselves except to a specific few. Our community is destined to disappear. We are all fated to be a blur just as I am in this foggy mirror. The broken fluorescent light flickers as the steam from my hot shower fades. I notice a small crack in the sliding mirror that distorts my face.

"I don't have any tolerance for squatters in this building!" said the Landlord.

"Stay focused," I said to myself. "Ignore his comments. He can't hurt you."

"What did you just say to me?"

I must have been louder than I thought. I need to get out of the shower. I realize the first step is the hardest but remaining motionless would define me even more than failure. I lift my leg out of the shower and plant it on the turquoise floor. The bathroom is warm from the shower, but the cold tiles send a jolt through my legs with each step. Turquoise colored tiles construct the space giving it the sense of a patient's room in an old hospital. This room is a relic from the past. I can relate. The smell of Head and Shoulders and body wash fills the area as I wipe beads of sweat from my face again. The reflection in the mirror is clouded by the shower's steam. Is this how I appear to others? Am I just someone who hides behind a barrier?

"You have some nerve taking up the shower for over three hours!" said the Landlord. "Who do you think you are?"

Who do you think you are? That is what he wants to know. He thinks he is somehow better than me just because he owns this building. The irony is that he has more in common with me than he might expect. We are both landlords of sorts but instead, I facilitate the lives that live inside this body. My tenants are filing complaints and I must show responsibility. I stare at the door which now rumbles in its frame as the Landlord knocks harder with each passing second. I see the reflection of my now aged Saturday persona, Nick Howell, in the doorknob. I guess my playboy persona took things a little too hard last night. Is that why I am having trouble remembering, or is it a reaction to something worse? I take a deep breath and calm myself down. I hear the growing murmur of voices from the hallway.

"Someone locked themselves in the bathroom?" said the first voice to the Landlord.

"It's probably that cocaine addict that hangs out right outside the building," said a second voice.

"Who's to say they aren't dead in there? That happened at my cousin's apartment building right off Jefferson Street," said yet another neighbor.

Each speculates the identity of the so called freak from the other side. They wait like viewers of an auto accident.

Their bickering mortifies me. I ignore the sounds and focus on the fog ridden mirror and the blurred figure that is staring at me.

"Sir, I am going to be late for church if I don't get in that bathroom now," said a new voice from outside the door.

"Dammit, John!" said the Landlord. "Can't you see I am trying to handle the situation the best I can? What do you want me to do? Bust the damn door down?

This confirms my suspicion of this apartment being owned by my default. Sunday is when I allow myself a day of rest from my other personas. I avoid eye contact with the man in the mirror. I can feel the tension in my neck grow by the second. Fear jolts through my body as I try to remember my default face.

Who do you think you are?

I reach into my garment bag, which was thrown on the floor hours ago in frustration, and grab a planner. I glance over to the daily calendar section and read through a novel's worth of text on each date, which only enhances my growing headache. At the bottom of the first page are detailed photos of each persona. Each picture looks more like a mugshot than a fond memory. The personas' wide-eyed glares keep the features at rest making it easy for me to mimic each blemish, eye color, and imperfection displayed on their face. Their corresponding names are written on each day to indicate which life I will be living on that particular date.

I must remember the details of up to six different personas. Maintaining various jobs and lives can be draining as I have seen each persona develop responsibilities, friends, and even relationships. It is important to keep these relationships as strictly casual because my other lives wouldn't allow for one to take on more of a leading role. Would I like to pursue a life with some of these people? Absolutely, but the choice of which simply is not in the cards. That being said, some of the more demanding personas can make me lose sight of who I truly am.

"Alright, asshole! You think you can walk in here, use our showers, live in our space without paying any rent?" the Landlord continues as he bangs louder. "All of that water you are using is causing water damage to the family in the apartment below you! I know that a squatter can't afford to fix that!"

Once again, I ignore the insult and bring my focus back to the task at hand. The last of the fog has just about dissipated from the mirror. I hear more footsteps from the outside of the door. The room is now only slightly warmer than usual. The hum from the ventilation continues to growl as it dissipates the fog. If I can only ask the Landlord what his occupant looks like. He would know my default form. A form that not only calls this apartment home but only comes out on Sunday.

Who am I?

I have lost something very personal. My true self is hidden underneath this body of clay. I look at myself in the mirror. The sad figure stares back as if he is trying to whisper a secret message with nothing but a glare. I can hear his message in my mind. My heart rate increases. *You're an outsider.* Sweat forms on my forehead. *Your community will no longer accept you.* My fists clench. *Asking for help is admitting defeat.* I slam my fists on the porcelain sink. The voices from outside the door grow silent for a split second. The planner falls to the floor showing all the appointments, names, and lives I am responsible for. I take a deep breath. Wipe the sweat from my face, clean up the floor, and accept defeat.

A common trick amongst Sculptors is to leave one aspect of yourself in each of your identities. That way you could trace yourself back to normal. The community calls this deconstructing. The stranger in the mirror lets out a sigh and begins changing my Saturday face, Nick Howell, into someone different. I begin to sculpt, as my name would imply. I start with my hair, the crown you can never take off. I work my comb through Nick's thick blond hair. With each pass of the comb my hair color ages roughly five years. It fades from Nick's blond to grey and gradually morphs into a vibrant white. This is a color of distinction that demands respect. It shows that I am a man who has aged gracefully rather than simply having some grey spots. I know this because my eldest persona, Liam Perry, dons this same hairstyle. He has always received more respect than any of my other identities.

Liam is a nice enough single 67-year-old man who spends one night a week acting as a volunteer security guard at the local art museum. The pieces, expertly placed on the wall reflect the dapperness of the man protecting them. No one, not even a child, would dare disappoint such a gentle yet rugged face by touching any of the art on display. Perhaps the saying is true. People respect their elders. This must be an inspiration from my true form. Why else would I make this so distinct?

After combing, I focus on my eyes and begin to blink rapidly. The color of my irises changes with each blink. Within a matter of seconds, I portray each color of the rainbow until I stop on the same cobalt blue that Nick knows so well. Say what you will about this playboy, and believe me I have a lot to say, but he knows how to have a good time. Nick is a bar rat who scuttles from pubs, taverns, nightclubs, to even invite only parties with a plus one using only his silver tongue to gain admittance. I make sure that Nick doesn't have any responsibilities so that he can enjoy all that life has to offer. I seem to remember him better than the other personas, which scares me. What if this is my destined role? The playboy partier. I'm not sure if my body or spirit could take his lifestyle every day. Either way, I have always been drawn to this color and feel that I must have chosen these with an eye on my past.

I then rub my nose as if I were giving it a massage. Each stroke flexes the bone into a new formation. My hands are like those of an artist molding in clay. I settle on a short, pointed nose with an exaggerated arch that belongs to my persona, Damian Harris. Is it that I don't find this arched nose attractive? Not necessarily, though many others don't. I follow this fear. Why should I transform myself for the pleasure of others? This ability should be for my pleasure, not those I interact with. This has shaped this persona, Damian, to be more self-conscious than the others. That is why I strategically placed him on Monday. I assume he would face less scrutiny on a day in which many don't pay close attention. It is probably why he spends his days hiding behind his computer writing about more interesting people as a freelance journalist. A mentality that I disagree with, but Damian believes wholeheartedly.

"I'll bust this door down! Do you hear me?" said the Landlord.

At this point, his threats are merely background noise for my work. I start rubbing my cheeks like a man trying to get warm out of fear of frostbite. My skin changes shades with time. Each shade of color provides a different experience, a different treatment from the world around me. I settle on a shade that best resembles the Latino heritage of Salazaar Martinez. This shade is very dear to my personal history as Salazar is my oldest persona. I vividly remember creating his appearance, his likes and dislikes, and even his penchant for music. A passion that leaves him spending his Friday nights practicing guitar. Someday I hope to see his name in lights. A logistical nightmare, but one I would gladly sacrifice for an old friend. It would be nice to fall into his life and stay permanently. I know he would take care of me in my old age. A life with him would be comfortable after years of stress. I pray that this is the case, but at the same time I feel so out of control.

I turn my focus to my ears. I begin to slightly pull them in all directions until I get the desired dimensions. After 10 minutes of shaping, I decide to revert back to the same ear shape that all of my personas have. Faced with endless possibilities and I still revert to the same look. Have I become a creature of habit? This reminds me of Lucas Danvers. A plain man, that was formed to be just so. I wanted a persona that would be easily manageable compared to those that came before him. He is referred to as the caretaker of our community mostly because he is the one who cleans, pays bills, and does any other unexciting work that simply none of the personas want to do. Perhaps I was lazy and simply reused traits, or maybe I was leaving myself a clue in plain sight. I follow this proverbial bread crumb and continue my work.

Lastly, there needs to be a small accent courtesy of my last alternate persona, named Amar Patel. His most identifying detail is the large scar on his face. I scratch the corner of my cheek and leave slight indentations above the scar to indicate where the stitches would be. This is painless and doesn't involve me mutilating my face, though it did take some practice until I got it just right. Amar tells stories from his experience as a zoo volunteer to anyone that will listen. In reality, he spends most of his shift as an assistant to the real zookeepers. Sure, he will occasionally participate in a live feeding, but most of his days are spent preparing food for the aviary, a job that doesn't seem nearly as exciting by comparison. Amar's ambitions are to someday work full time at the zoo rather than simply volunteering his time, which of course is impossible when you are only available to work one day a week. I have always felt bad about this. I will make it up to him some day. Either way, Amar's visual scar gives him a rich backstory that made him very engaging to others and provides a nice finishing touch to a work of art.

Among all the commotion outside the door, I find myself in a meditative state due to my creative expression. I take a step back to see the face I have created. This stranger stands in the mirror and gives a curious look as if my reflection is slowly analyzing each detail written on my face. Who is this person staring back? My face appears to be a composite of each person combined into one unique face. The quest for my default has left me with an appearance that seems alien yet intimate. Like someone you recognize but don't know from where. Could this truly be who I am? Did my deconstruction work? Will I be accepted by the larger community of Sculptors? I finish my ritual by brushing my teeth and eventually cleaning up the countertop, though not too well.

Suddenly, I feel a massive slam against the door. The locks break and the knob flies into the adjacent wall shattering a portion of the tile. I quickly cover my privates with a towel which still doesn't leave much to the imagination. I hear the Landlord yell my name, which proves that the process was a success. I feel a sense of relief as I realize that I have not reached the point of no return. He continues to berate me about apparent water damage caused by my endless shower. Others lose interest when they don't see my helpless body on the floor and slowly migrate back to their homes. The Landlord calms himself and explains his warnings and multiple fines I will need to pay as a result of this episode. As I exit the bathroom, I take one final look at my reflection.

Who am I?

Does real life inspire art, or is it art that inspires real life? Perhaps it's a constant circling process of art inspiring life and vice versa. I accept who I am, but also who they are. Each appearance, each experience, each small detail forms a larger whole. My never-ending mixture of lives and experiences is represented in this face here.

The friend in the mirror smiles at me. There is a sense of comfortability in this face but with enough mystery to leave you at a distance. It's as if we haven't seen each other in years but are picking up right where we left off. This man is an enigma that I have known my whole life. The tension in my muscles fades away with the remaining steam. My default appearance isn't important. The thoughts of the Sculptor community are just as insignificant. This community from within me has shown more support than they ever have. Today I had a crisis. Where were the other sculptors to help me? Would they even have come if I asked them to? I would like to think they would, but deep down I know they are just as busy. The only ones who were there for me, who have always been there for me, are the identities that I have constructed. They helped guide me back home knowing it was in the best interest of their larger group. I find comfort in six drastically different men who would never have any business with one another. I am the glue that holds together their lives, not the other way around. I have spent my whole life changing and shifting into someone different but have never attempted to change my own mindset. I smile at my friend in the mirror and ask one last time.

Who am I?

Both the stranger in the mirror and myself respond in unison.

I am the community of me.

The Train to Piper Hollow
by Jen Mierisch

Jen Mierisch's dream job is to write Twilight Zone *episodes, but until then, she's a website administrator by day and a writer of odd stories by night. Jen's work can be found in* Horla, Dark Moments, HAVOK, *and various short story anthologies. Jen can be found haunting her local library just outside Chicago, USA. Read more at www.jenmierisch.com.*

I angled my chin toward the campfire, hoping its light was casting spooky shadows across my face.

"And then," I said, "the man says to the old couple, 'Do you know a young woman named Jane, with red hair and a tattoo on her arm? She was hitchhiking, and I picked her up earlier tonight. She gave me this address. But then she disappeared.'"

On the other side of the blaze, my best friend Jason turned the stick to bronze his marshmallow. He looked a little bored. Maybe he'd heard this one before.

"And the old folks look at each other, and they go really pale." I popped the last of my s'more into my mouth, licked chocolate off my fingers, and sat up straight, winding up for the final pitch. "Finally," I said, "the old woman says, 'Jane was our daughter. She died in a car accident *twenty years ago tonight.*'"

"Nice one, Court," Jason said. He didn't look scared at all. I frowned.

The summer sun was pretty much gone now, the horizon a deep indigo. Across the yard, my house loomed black against the starry sky. I watched the lone light switch off; my mom had gone to bed. Had it gotten colder? I scooted closer to the fire. Jason would tease me if he saw me shiver.

Jason sandwiched the gooey marshmallow between two graham crackers, withdrew the stick, and chomped. Crumbs cascaded toward the lawn. We'd done several campfires this summer, ever since Jason learned how to build a fire with his Scout troop. Not for the first time, I felt a pang of envy.

"When are you leaving for Scout camp again?" I asked him.

"Saturday," he said. "Camp is gonna be awesome this year!"

"How long is it for?"

"Two weeks!"

"Lucky," I said. "I wish I could go."

"Sorry, Court. It's *Boy* Scout camp. No girls allowed," he said through a mouthful of marshmallow. "It's not like your Little League team."

"I'm the fastest runner on that team," I pointed out. "And the third-best hitter." Girls had been allowed in Little League for ages, but I was the only girl on my team. Even though I knew I was good enough to compete, it seemed like I was always having to prove it.

Jason shrugged. "You could join Girl Scouts."

"It's not the same," I said. Truth was, we didn't have the money for both Little League and Scouts, so the point was moot. I sighed. "It'll be totally boring here without you."

"Whatcha gonna do while I'm gone?" he asked me. "Hang out at the *mall* with Emily?"

"Gag me!" I said. "I'd rather watch grass grow." Emily, our neighborhood pal since preschool, had recently spurned tree climbing and tag in favor of makeup and *Teen Beat* magazine. I hadn't hung out at her house since the day she'd complained that my hair was too short for her crimping iron.

Jason laughed, scooped up a couple of marshmallows that had fallen onto the grass, and stuffed them into his face.

"I might have a babysitting job, actually," I said. "For little Mandy down the street." I stretched and yawned. "Other than that, I'll probably just play Colecovision for two weeks. Although it'll only take me, like, fifteen minutes to beat your high score on *Zaxxon*."

"You wish!" He sat up, opened his mouth, and expelled an epic belch.

"Gross!" I told him.

"My turn for stories," said Jason. "I got a good one for ya." He wiggled his eyebrows.

"Is this another Amazing Stories episode that you're gonna pretend you made up?" I said, smirking.

"Nope," he said. "This one's a true story. And it happened right here in this town." He leaned over and switched off my transistor radio, cutting off Madonna in the middle of "Live to Tell."

In the sudden quiet, the crickets' chirping sounded like chalk screeching across a blackboard. I drew up my knees and hugged them. The flickering flames reflected in Jason's eyes as he began.

"A hundred years ago," he said, "there was a little girl named Julia. Her mother abandoned her, and her father died of dysentery."

"Dysentery?" I laughed. "Like in that game *Oregon Trail?*"

"Yup. He pooped himself to death," said Jason. I rolled my eyes.

"Anyways," he continued, "little Julia was an orphan now. She survived by drinking from scummy ponds, stealing clothes off people's laundry lines, and eating whatever frogs and rats she could catch."

"Grody to the max," I said.

"Hey, when you're starving, you do what you gotta do. Julia was only six, but she was faster than a cheetah. She'd catch the rats with her teeth and swing them around by the tail to get rid of the flies, and then she ate 'em raw."

I stretched my head to the side and fake-barfed.

"So, Julia went to an orphanage, but she hated it there. They made her clean the headmaster's boots with her tongue and muck out the horse stalls with her bare hands. She kept hoping somebody would adopt her, but nobody wanted a rat-eating thief, so she was out of luck.

"There was this one train that ran through town. The exact same train tracks that run behind our school today. Every day Julia would wander over to those tracks and wait for that train to come by. She would just stand there and stare at it, because more than anything she wanted to get on that train and go away from her miserable life.

"One day, when Julia was watching the train, she saw a beautiful woman in the window. The woman wore this shiny, brightly colored dress, and Julia felt shy, because all she ever wore was nasty gray rags. The woman waved. And Julia was happy, because nobody ever waved to her, they spit on her. Then, as the train passed, the woman called out something to Julia."

"What?"

"She said, 'Three more days.'"

To hide my shivering, I stabbed a marshmallow and aimed the stick at the fire.

"The next day, the woman was there again. She called out to Julia, 'Two more days.'" And Julia knew the woman meant that she could get on the train too.

"Next day, the lady said, 'One more day,' with a great big smile. And on the last day, Julia put on her best rags and waited by the tracks. Right on schedule, the train came chugging along. This time, the woman was leaning out the door and reaching out her arms. Julia grabbed on, and the lady pulled her inside. She landed on the floor of the train, and she was so excited. But then she looked up at the lady's face. She wasn't beautiful anymore. Her face was all rotted, like a leper, with pieces of cheek missing, showing her teeth through the gaps. She had no eyes, just two black holes, like someone had gouged out her eyeballs."

Deciding against that third s'more, I tossed the stick into the fire, marshmallow and all.

"Julia screamed and tried to run, but it was too late. The other passengers were coming over, and they were rotted too. They got closer and closer. And then they ate Julia for dinner, starting with her hands. One finger a time." Jason put a finger in his mouth, then another, sucking each one with a loud slurp.

"Bad luck for Julia," he said. "The woman on the train was queen of the zombies, and zombies can only survive for so long without a taste of human flesh. So every year in August, that train comes back, and it rides right through our town. And if some kid gets lost, or if their parents kick them out, and they wander too close to the tracks, the zombie queen will be there waiting to give them a ride to hell." He sat back, grinning triumphantly.

"Omigod, Jason," I said. "That is so sick."

"One finger at a time!" He waggled his fingers at my face. I shrieked and swatted them away.

He checked our stash. "Aww. We're out of Hershey bars. Want to finish the crackers?" He broke the last graham cracker and held out half. I shook my head rapidly.

"You're really spooked," he declared.

"Am not."

"Yeah, you are!" he crowed.

"Shut up," I said. "Maybe you can scare the other Cub Scouts with that story, but not me."

"*Boy* Scouts," he corrected me. "After fifth grade we're not Cubs anymore." He tossed a marshmallow into the air and caught it in his mouth.

Ten minutes later, Jason was snoring in his pup tent, and I was lying wide awake in mine, listening to the racket of the cicadas. A ways off, the lonesome call of a train whistle echoed across the fields.

Shonda Pierce, I recalled suddenly. She had been in the same class as Jason's big sister Wendy. Last summer, she had run away from home, and no one had seen her since. Old Mr. Bartlow at the convenience store was apparently the last one to see Shonda. He said he saw her walking down by the railroad tracks.

I pictured a decaying face and monstrous teeth chewing on a girl's fingers, making crunching sounds as they cut through bones, sending painted fingernails clattering to the ground.

Pulling my sleeping bag up over my head, I squeezed my eyes shut. I wanted to run to the house, jump into my bed, and pull up my bedspread until every last inch of my skin was covered.

With one hand, I groped for my flashlight, pulled it inside the sleeping bag, and flipped its plastic switch, instantly feeling both relief and shame. Jason didn't need a nightlight, like some wimpy little kid. Why did I? I knew what he'd call me, if he could see. *Scaredy-cat.*

"Our cat is a jag-wire," said Mandy, scrambling up the hill after me. Beneath her sneakers, the dust rose and hung in the hot summer air.

I rolled my eyes. "It's *jaguar,* not *jag-wire.* And nobody has a jaguar as a pet."

"We do!" she insisted.

"Oh, yeah? Where'd you get it?"

She stuck her chin up and frowned at me. "From the zoo!"

Mandy lived a couple houses down. We didn't usually hang out. Almost-sixth-graders don't play with six-year-olds. But Mandy's mom had asked me to babysit while her grandma was in the hospital. With Jason gone at camp, I was bored stiff, and hey, a dollar an hour was a dollar an hour.

"Have you gone across this bridge before?" I asked. We stood at the edge of the abandoned train trestle that crossed over the Weser River. Far below us, the water churned and flowed, hurtling over rugged rocks.

"Yeah! A million times!" she said, eyeballing the crumbling wood beams.

"Let's go, then." I tugged aside the rusted chain-link fence.

Mandy followed, stepping carefully from one beam to the next, arms held out for balance. Her eyes darted down, glancing between the planks at the roaring water. But she found her footing, her grimy sneakers gripping the steel spikes and tarnished metal plates next to the rails.

At the end of the bridge, Mandy jumped down after me, grinning, her face flushed with success. I gave her a high-five. The kid might have an overactive imagination, but she wasn't chicken.

That's when we heard the drone of the train's horn. We looked over at the brand-new steel-and-concrete bridge, two hundred feet away from the old wreck we'd just crossed.

The afternoon was starting to get foggy, and at first the train was invisible, just the sound of the engine indicating its approach. The headlights appeared first, then the huge metal body followed, bells chiming as it emerged from the mist. It streamed across the new bridge, all clanking metal and rushing wind, and raced across the field in front of us, winding around the bend like a silver snake.

Mandy waved at the train. "Courtney, did you see those people?" she asked. "They waved to me!"

"What people? That was a freight train," I said.

"There was a lady," she said. "A pretty lady. Wearing a big blue hat."

Right, I thought. *And you have a pet jaguar.*

"Whatever. Let's walk back across the new bridge," I said, striding off toward it.

A couple of days later, Mandy slapped her hand over the top of her plastic cup, stood up from the riverbank, and ran over to where I was sitting on the grass. "I got one!" she announced.

I peeked into it. "Cool." The frog extended its slimy legs and hopped. Mandy giggled and flattened her hand to block the amphibian's escape.

"Take it home," I suggested. "Keep it as a pet." I resumed tossing stones into the water, watching the minnows scatter and swerve.

"Nah," she said. "Mack would never let me." She got quiet then, taking the frog between her cupped hands and petting it gently with a fingertip.

A horn blared, echoing against the riverbanks. We looked up and watched the train barreling across the concrete bridge.

"Courtney," Mandy asked me, "where does that train go?"

"I don't know."

"That lady was there again. Didn't you see her? She went like this." Mandy waved her hands as if to say *come here.*

"Oh, I get it," I said. "Very funny. You've heard that story too. About the train and the little orphan girl. Who told you that story? It's too gross for a little kid."

Her brow furrowed. "What are you talking about? What story?"

That night, I asked Mom where the train went. She was hunched over her checkbook at the kitchen table, rubbing her temple with one hand and flipping through bills with the other. "What train, honey?" she said, not looking up.

"It goes over the Weser River bridge," I said. "Is it Amtrak?" My dad used to talk about taking me on an Amtrak train ride, all the way to Chicago. Maybe he would, one day, when he wasn't so busy driving trucks.

She looked up. "I'm not sure," she said. Her smile seemed small. "Might be that private line that runs up to Piper Hollow."

"Piper Hollow?"

"That fancy resort up in the hills." She rolled her eyes. Most of us regular folks in little old Hamlin, Ohio, went camping, or on road trips, if we went on vacation at all. Resorts were for uppity city people with gobs of money to spend on croquet, or polo, or whatever rich people did.

So it might be a passenger train after all. I hadn't seen any people on it. But apparently Mandy had, and someone had seen her, too.

Friday, I had the day to myself. Mack was working night shifts, Mandy's mom had told me, so he'd be home.

That afternoon, after baseball practice, I approached a couple of my buddies from the team. "Hey," I said. "Want to come over and play video games?"

"Nah, I gotta get home," said Brian.

"Yeah, me too," added Tony, kicking the dirt. They turned and walked off together.

I watched several teammates pile into the back of a pickup truck, laughing and shouting as it drove off. Alone, I wandered toward the river.

As I scrambled down the bank, I noticed movement up on the abandoned train trestle. Mandy, who had apparently crossed it all by herself, waved to me as she came back across. I smiled. She was pretty gutsy for a pipsqueak kid. I wondered if Mack knew she was gone.

"Courtney, guess what!" she said, squeezing through the gap in the fence and running over to me. "The train came again. And that lady talked to me!"

I sighed.

"She said they're going to a party! They're gonna have cake and ice cream, and play games."

"Oh?" I said, playing along. "And what was she wearing this time?"

"A pretty dress, all different colors," she said, "with buttons all the way up to here." She reached a dirty hand up to her throat.

"Doesn't sound like a party dress to me."

"She's just fancy," Mandy said. "That's what I call her. Miss Fancy."

I chuckled.

"Shut up!" she shouted. "Don't laugh at Miss Fancy. She's my friend."

I watched Mandy stomp off. After a minute, I turned and followed her.

She'd gotten as far as the front yard when I heard the noise from inside. Glass smashed and people hollered. Mandy stopped in her tracks and seemed to shrink.

At the side of the house, a screen door banged open. Out came Mandy's mom and a big angry man, still arguing. Her mom marched toward the Chevette parked in the driveway. He shouted curses as she backed out and peeled off down the street.

I heard a door slam. Mandy had skittered through the front door. Through the window, I glimpsed her blonde head as she scurried out of sight.

The angry man tramped back toward the house. He was as big as Sloth in *The Goonies* and almost as ugly. "What're you looking at?" he snarled at me.

I turned and ran.

Saturday morning, I saw Mandy sitting at the edge of the playground, playing with My Little Ponies. She was hard to miss, decked out like she was, in a bright red silky blouse with ruffles at the neck, several sizes too big for her.

"Don't you look dressy," I observed.

"It's for the party," she said, tying a bow in Applejack's mane.

"Whose party?"

"Miss Fancy's. She invited me. It's tonight!"

I couldn't take it anymore. "You know, you need to stop lying."

Her little mouth hung open as she stared at me.

"Don't you know about the boy who cried wolf?" I said. Why did I care so much if she lied or not? Was this how it felt to be a big sister?

"I am not lying!" she yelled.

"It's not real, Mandy," I said, trying to make my voice softer, like my mom's. "I don't know who told you that story about the lady on the train. But it's just a story."

Mandy jumped to her feet. "It is not!" she insisted. "Miss Fancy is real. She said I should come with her. She says the train goes to a beautiful land where everybody's happy!" Scowling, she seized her ponies and stormed off. As she rounded the corner, I thought I could hear her crying.

That afternoon, I was watching the Reds game on TV when I heard the gunshot.

Mom looked up from her magazine, squinted through the window, then hurried out the door. When I saw where she was going, I ran out to follow her. A rusty Ford pickup truck zoomed down the street in the opposite direction. I recognized Mack's face at the wheel.

I saw Mandy's next-door neighbor first, Mr. Garraway, leaning against his porch railing. He was shaking his head and mumbling, "He shot her. The bastard shot her." Mom came out of Mandy's house and shouted to Mr. Garraway, "Their phone's not working. Call an ambulance!" He hustled inside.

A flicker caught my eye. Behind the houses, across the field, somebody wearing red was running toward the woods.

I didn't think. I just took off across the grass. Stumbling over scrubby weeds, I kept an eye on that red shirt as it darted between the trees and emerged into the field behind our elementary school.

My heart was thumping, my breath coming in gasps, but I had nearly caught up to her. Mandy had stopped at the bend in the railroad tracks, her back to me. Up ahead, the silver train blared its lonesome horn as it chugged toward us.

One of the train car's doors was open. A woman in a multicolored dress leaned out of it, smiling, beckoning. Reaching out her hands, Mandy stepped toward the tracks. The train sped closer, slowing as it reached the bend. The woman stretched out both arms. I was too far away. I wasn't going to make it.

Summoning one final burst of speed, I sprinted forward, grabbed Mandy around the waist, and pulled her away. "No!" she screamed, kicking furiously at me. "Let me go! I want to go with Miss Fancy. I don't want to be here anymore!"

The train had slowed to a crawl. The woman was no longer smiling. She stretched out a long white hand, with long fingernails painted scarlet, and snatched at Mandy's arm. I yanked Mandy away, but not before those nails scratched bloody trails on her wrist. The woman screeched like a wild animal. I looked up, and I nearly screamed myself. Her face had shriveled like a rotten apple. Bones poked through withered skin, her snarling lips bared pointed teeth, and her eyes were nothing but black-shadowed sockets.

The train bucked and rattled as it thundered past, carrying away that horrible face, that unearthly howling. I set Mandy down and collapsed to my knees. Mandy must have seen it too, because she clung to me, trembling, burying her face against my neck as the train puffed into the woods and vanished.

Jason got back from camp on a Saturday. He came into my bedroom while Mandy and I were dancing to the radio.

"We built this city!" I sang.

"We built this city on rock and rooooolllll!" Mandy crooned, executing a wide twirl, as if rolling in midair.

We grabbed hands and spun, hurtling faster and faster until we collapsed to the rug in a giggling heap.

Jason leaned against the doorframe, shaking his head and smiling.

"Mandy," someone called from down the hall.

"Mom!" Mandy started toward my bedroom door, halted midstride, pivoted, and ran back to me. She hugged me tightly around the waist. "Bye, Courtney," she said.

"Come over tomorrow, so we can play catch again," I told her.

"Okay," she said, smiling. Then she made a beeline out the door, passing Jason like he wasn't even there.

I went to my boom box and turned the volume down. "You're back! How was camp?"

"Awesome," he said, and launched enthusiastically into tales of high ropes courses, canoeing, and playing Spies in the Woods. I listened, twisting the caps back on the nail polish jars I'd borrowed from my mom.

"Nice nails," he said, looking at my rainbow-painted fingers. They looked like a kindergarten art project.

"Thanks," I said.

"Did Mandy paint those?"

"One finger at a time," I said, waggling them in his face.

Jason chuckled. "So," he said next, "what'd you end up doing for two weeks?"

I opened my mouth, and then closed it again.

I thought about our last campfire, when I'd worried if he'd laugh at me for turning a light on in the dark.

Through the window, I watched Mandy walk across the lawn with her mom, who was limping, using a crutch to support her injured leg. It's a good thing Mack was a bad shot, Mom had said. We didn't see him around anymore.

"Baseball," I answered, finally. "And babysitting."

Jason's eyes lit up. "I heard the gnarliest ghost story at camp about a babysitter," he said. "Want to do a fire tonight?"

"Definitely," I said.

He rubbed his hands together. "Great. It's a really good one."

"Sure."

"I can't wait to see your face," he said. "You're gonna be scared stiff."

I looked at him and grinned. "I think I can handle it."

Made in the USA
Middletown, DE
28 May 2024